BULLET
TRAIN
DISASTER

For the musicians, groupies, and roadies of the
Ginninderra Wind Orchestra. Rock on!

STERLING CHILDREN'S BOOKS
New York

An Imprint of Sterling Publishing Co., Inc.
1166 Avenue of the Americas
New York, NY 10036

Text © 2016 Jack Heath
Interior illustrations © 2016 Scholastic Australia
Cover © 2020 Sterling Publishing Co., Inc.

Previously published by Scholastic Australia in 2016

ISBN 978-1-4549-3844-6

Library of Congress Cataloging-in-Publication Data

Names: Heath, Jack, 1986– author.
Title: Bullet train disaster / Jack Heath.
Description: New York : Sterling Publishing Co., Inc., [2020] | Series:
  Choose your destiny ; 1 "Previously published by Scholastic Australia in
  2016." | Audience: Ages 8–12. (provided by Sterling Publishing Co., Inc.)
  | Summary: On the disastrous first trip of a new bullet train that ascends
  nearly vertically up steep Mount Grave, the reader makes choices that
  determine how the hero proceeds––and whether survival is possible.
Identifiers: LCCN 2019055967| ISBN 9781454938446 (paperback) | ISBN
  9781454938477 (epub)
Subjects: LCSH: Plot-your-own stories. | CYAC: Survival––Fiction. | Adventure
  and adventurers––Fiction. | High speed trains––Fiction. | Plot-your-own
  stories.
Classification: LCC PZ7.H3478 Bul 2020 | DDC [Fic]––dc23 LC record available at https://lccn.loc.gov_2019055967

For information about custom editions, special sales, and premium and corporate purchases, please contact
Sterling Special Sales at 800-805-5489 or specialsales@sterlingpublishing.com.

Manufactured in Canada

Lot #:
2 4 6 8 10 9 7 5 3 1
03/20

sterlingpublishing.com

Cover design by Julie Robine

Cover art by Pete Ware.
Snow mountain range © vichie81 | Shutterstock.com; Digital clock © Samarskaya | iStockphoto.com

JACK HEATH

BULLET TRAIN DISASTER

STERLING CHILDREN'S BOOKS

New York

It doesn't look like any train you've ever seen.

It has the usual parts—sliding doors, plastic windows, massive, grinding wheels—but it's facing *up*. The mountain is so steep that the rails are almost vertical. How is that supposed to work? It's only one car long, but still. Can trains even go uphill?

Despite the strangeness, it seems familiar. As if you have taken a ride on it before. Unsettled, you glance at your watch. Wasn't the train supposed to depart an hour ago?

The other passengers seem as baffled as you feel. They all look as though they've just awakened, and are surprised to find themselves here. Everyone except Pigeon.

"This is going to be awesome," Pigeon says, hopping from foot to foot on the platform. Her brown boots are too big for her and her wool jacket is inside out, showing off the cool patterns in the lining. Her purple-streaked hair sticks out in tufts from under her beanie.

Her real name is Paige, but everyone calls her Pigeon because she's curious about *everything*. You've been friends with her forever. When you won the ticket— "You and a friend can be first to ride the new bullet train up Mount Grave!"—it only took two seconds to decide whom to invite.

"You think it's safe?" you ask.

"Of course! They wouldn't be letting people on if it wasn't."

You're not so sure. The website looked very professional, with pictures of everything from the train conductor's controls, to the lookout on the mountaintop. But now that you're here, you see that the staff bustling back and forth all wear running shoes. The security guards have bloodshot eyes and rumpled uniforms. The signs on the walls have spelling mistakes. And Mount Grave looks really, really high. Black clouds coil around the peak like smoke. The cliffs are leopard-spotted with snow. In the stunted trees halfway up, crows dart from one withered branch to another.

"The train has never had a single crash," Pigeon adds.

"This is the first trip," you say.

"You know what I mean. They've tested it."

You're not sure how she knows that, but you say nothing.

"All aboard!" the conductor yells, his black cap low over his eyes, a manic grin on his round face. He sounds like he's been looking forward to saying those words.

A dark rumbling fills the air. The platform vibrates beneath your feet. Maybe it's the engine of the train warming up. Maybe not.

Pigeon joins the line of passengers. "Are you coming, or what?"

"I'm coming," you say.

Go to the next page.

You line up behind Pigeon. Ahead of you, an old woman glares at the train and tightens a silk scarf over her drooping mouth. A lanky man in a broad-brimmed hat fiddles with his video camera. A boy is dressed in ski gear and carrying a snowboard. Ice clogs the creases of his outfit, as if this is his second trip up the mountain today.

Pigeon seems more excited than any of the other passengers. When the train gets to the top, she plans to search for some super-rare—and super-deadly—giant ticks that supposedly live up there. She thinks she'll be famous if she can prove they exist.

A burly security guard glowers at you from a distance, one hand on his earpiece. You look around, but no one is behind you. It's definitely you the guard is looking at. Why? You haven't done anything.

You nudge Pigeon. "See that guy?"

"What guy?" she asks, too loudly.

"*Shh.* The security guard."

By the time Pigeon looks, the guard has already turned away. "What about him?"

"He was looking at us."

She grins. "What did you steal?"

"Nothing!"

"I'm kidding." She elbows your ribs. "Relax. Soon you'll be on top of the tallest mountain in the world. He won't be able to see you from up there."

You frown. "Isn't Mount Everest taller?"

"Depends how you measure it. Everest is higher above sea level."

"How do *you* measure it?"

She flashes a wicked grin. "By how long it takes to hit the ground if you fall off the top."

Another guard—a beak-nosed woman with watery eyes—takes Pigeon's ticket and says, "Thank you, Miss Nguyen. Your seat is by the window, five rows up on your left."

Pigeon steps into the train and disappears around the corner.

You reach into your pocket for your ticket.

A hand grabs your arm. It's the beefy security guard who was staring at you before.

"Are you Taylor?" he asks.

If you say, "Neil Taylor, that's me," go to the next page.
If you tell him, "No, I'm Shelley Black," go to page 8.

"Neil Taylor, that's me," you say. "What can I do for you?"

The guard sighs. "No, I'm looking for Taylor Morton. Do you know him?"

You shake your head and glance at the rest of the line. "What does he look like?"

"I'm not sure," the guard admits.

He says something else, but you're distracted. A man in a brown golf cap is skulking around the platform. Could he be a passenger? If so, why isn't he getting on board?

The man sees you looking and walks briskly away.

"Who is this Taylor Morton?" you ask. "And why is there so much security?"

"Because of the bandits," the guard says. "This train is made from valuable metals. In fact—" A nervous look crosses his face, as if he knows he's said too much. "Just get on board, Mr. Taylor. You're holding up the line."

You shuffle up the stairs into the train. The inside is completely bizarre. The slope is so steep that there are stairs instead of an aisle. The seats have complicated harnesses, like you'd expect to see on a rocket ship. Passengers are throwing gear into overhead lockers, where it won't bounce around while the train is moving. The whole car smells like bleach. You wonder if one of the test operators threw up and the floor needed to be cleaned. Climbing the stair-aisle feels the same as approaching the top of a waterslide.

You find Pigeon about halfway up the car, fiddling with her harness. "Stupid seatbelt," she mutters. "Why does it need so many buckles?"

"Because the train goes at 300 miles per hour," you say.

She jumps. "Neil! Don't sneak up on me like that."

"It's true—I'm a ninja."

She glances at her watch. "Pretty slow, for a ninja. What took you so long?"

Turn to page 10.

"**N**o," you tell the guard. "I'm Shelley Black."

"Oh." He releases your arm. "Sorry, Miss Black. May I see your ticket?"

You hand it over. He inspects it.

"That person you were with . . ."

"She isn't Taylor either," you say. Clearly he's looking for someone he's never met.

The guard looks at the ticket checker. She confirms this with a nod.

"Who's Taylor?" you ask the guard. "Why are you looking for her?"

He shrugs. "I don't know. I just got a message: *Tell Taylor Morton not to get on the train.* But none of the female passengers are named Taylor." He frowns. "Taylor *is* a girl's name, right?"

"Not always," you say.

He groans and gives your ticket back. "Never mind. Have a safe journey."

He walks away, shaking his head.

"Why is there so much security?" you ask the ticket checker.

"Defense department restrictions," she says.

You look around. You don't see anyone who looks

military. "What does the defense department have to do with this train?"

"That's classified." The ticket checker waves you onto the train.

The inside of the train is surreal. The slope is so steep that there are stairs instead of an aisle. Lighting strips line the ceiling, like on an airplane. You can smell rocket fuel sizzling in the engine. Heating vents drone above the seats.

You're worn out by the time you've climbed the stairs up to your row, where Pigeon is fiddling with her five-point harness. "Stupid seatbelt," she mutters. "Why does it need so many straps?"

"I think we're about to find out," you say.

She jumps. "Shelley! Where have you been?"

Go to the next page.

"**T**hat security guard I told you about," you say. "He wanted to ask me a question."

"What question?"

You're about to respond when the conductor's voice crackles over the PA. "We're almost ready to get underway," he says. "In tests, this train was able to accelerate to its full speed in thirty-six seconds, but we'll take four minutes instead to minimize the risk of, uh . . ." He mumbles something.

"Did he just say 'broken neck?'" Pigeon whispers.

"Or 'smoking wreck'—" A roar drowns out the rest of your reply as the train lurches into motion. The force pushes you down into your seat. Other passengers scream. Now you know why they call it a bullet train— it feels as if the train has been fired from a gun. You're hurtling up the mountain at a dangerous speed.

The platform vanishes from the windows. A dramatic skyline swooshes into view, littered with the spikes of other brutal mountains. It feels like your stomach has been crushed into a tiny ball.

You think you see something between the trees. A dark shape against the snow. A person—no. Too tall, too wide to be a person.

The figure is gone before you can get a better look.

"We're going really fast!" Pigeon yells over the thundering wheels.

"I noticed," you shout.

The train swerves left up a bend in the tracks. Some commotion up the front of the train catches your eye. The kid wearing ski clothes evidently wasn't buckled in properly. The turn has knocked him out of his seat, and now he's clinging to the seatback as the train goes faster and faster. His eyes are wide with terror. If he loses his grip, he'll go flying through the train.

"Help!" he screams.

One of his hands slips off the seat. He's going to fall.

The guy seated next to him grabs for the boy's hand, but the angle isn't right. He can't quite reach with his seatbelt fastened, and he isn't willing to release it.

You could catch the boy as he hurtles past—but you'd have to unbuckle your own seatbelt to stretch out far enough. What do you do?

If you release your buckle to catch the falling boy, go to page 14.
If you stay belted in while you reach for him, go to page 17.

01:05

"**M**e?" Pigeon demands. "Why am I going first?"

You don't want to leave your oldest friend trapped in a shrinking train as a giant blade hacks off more and more of it. But you can't find the words to explain that right now.

"Just go!" you shout.

The guillotine rises out of sight. Trusting you, Pigeon throws herself through the gap—

Just in time. The enormous blade comes crashing back down, slicing off another segment of the train and narrowly missing Pigeon's feet. She lands on all fours between the rails outside.

It's your turn. The guillotine rises up. You run and leap toward the outside world—

The blade swooshes down from above you, shrieking as it rips through the train walls.

Something hits your foot—

And then the ground rushes up to meet you.

Wham! You find yourself lying facedown against the gravel in the rail bed, breathing heavily. Your face hurts. And your hands, and your knees. But you're alive.

You twist your head and look back at your feet, making sure they're still there. They are, but the sole of one shoe has been sliced off. If you had jumped a split-second later, you would have stumps for ankles.

"Are you OK?" Pigeon asks.

You nod, too shaken to speak. Behind you the chopper is noisily turning the rest of the train into valuable scrap metal.

"Hey!" Pigeon yells. She's looking up and waving her arms. "Down here!"

You follow her gaze. A helicopter circles above you, but it's not the bandits. The word *POLICE* is printed on the side.

You stand on aching legs and join Pigeon, shouting and waving. It looks like everything's going to be OK.

00:00

You survived! There are ten other ways to escape the danger—try to find them all!

21:20

Just as the boy loses his grip on the seatback, you release your own buckle. The harness pops open.

"What are you doing?" Pigeon shrieks.

You ignore her. The boy hurtles past, grabbing at the air. You reach out for him.

Success! You grab his wrist and he grabs yours—but instead of hauling him to safety, you get pulled out of your seat. Suddenly you're both tumbling down through the train, sweeping dizzily past the other passengers, the universe lurching around you.

The boy slams into the rear door of the train, shoulder first. You crash into him. His ski gear dulls the impact, but the wind is still knocked out of you.

The train keeps accelerating. The force pins you down. The boy tries to push you off him, but as he moves, one of his hands bumps the *EMERGENCY OPEN* button.

"No!" you cry, but too late. The door whooshes open. You both tumble out of the train into the cold daylight. You glimpse the tracks rushing past beneath you, before—

Wham! You and the boy smash down onto the rails. The impact leaves you stunned, your stomach swirling and your ears ringing.

You're lucky. Because you were flying backward as the train was speeding forward, you didn't hit the tracks very fast—and because you landed on top of the boy again, his protective clothing saved your life.

Still, when the world stops spinning, your whole body hurts. Every inch of skin feels bruised.

"I say!" the boy wheezes. His voice bounces off the distant peak. He sounds British, and probably rich.

You look at him. He's sprawled on his back, staring up at the sky, a big grin on his red-cheeked face. He has a straight nose, narrow shoulders and high, thin eyebrows that almost look penciled on.

"I say!" he says again. "Incredible."

You sit up, groaning as all your joints protest. "We nearly died!" you say.

"Piffle." The boy waves a hand. "We're fine."

He stands up and brushes some snow off his clothes.

"Fine?" You gesture at the wasteland of dead trees and frozen rocks around you. The skeleton of a wild animal is sprawled in the distance. "We're stranded halfway up a mountain!"

"And me without my snowboard," the boy agrees gloomily. "Can you imagine riding these rails back down the hill? It would be marvelous!"

Your teeth chatter. Your jacket is too thin to keep out the cold. How long will you survive out here?

You reach into your pocket for your phone. But it's

shattered into a thousand jagged pieces that prick your fingertips. Your compass seems to be intact, but other than telling you which way north is, it won't do much good.

"I should introduce myself, I suppose," the boy says. He sticks out his gloved hand. "Taylor Morton, at your service."

Go to page 19.

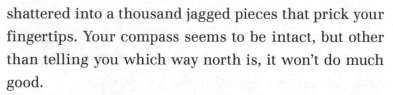

You fling out a hand, trying to catch the falling boy. The seatbelt bites into your shoulders and hips. But even with your fingertips outstretched, the boy remains out of reach. He tumbles past, a blur of hair and clothes and wild eyes, before he slams into the back of the train.

"Hit the brakes!" you scream. "Stop the train!"

Too late. The rear door whooshes open—the boy must have hit the emergency button when he fell. He rolls out into the daylight and disappears.

The wind roars at the open door. The brakes squeal, and you're thrown forward against the seatbelt. Everyone is yelling.

The train was going so fast that by the time it eventually stops, you feel like you must be miles away from where the boy fell out. You're halfway up the mountain. If you weren't so scared, the view from the window would be enchanting.

"Are you OK?" Pigeon asks. She's breathing heavily. Some spit is dotted on her chin. Hopefully it isn't yours—you were screaming pretty loudly.

"I'm all right," you say. "You?"

"Yeah, I'm fine." She looks back at the open door. "Do you think that kid is OK?"

It seems unlikely. The train had been going very fast.

"I tried to save him," you say. It's the truth, but it feels like a lie. You could have done more.

"Ladies and gentlemen." The conductor's voice comes over the PA. He sounds shaken. "I've engaged the emergency brake. I'm going to have to ask you all to disembark while I inspect the train."

"What?" the old woman in the silk scarf shouts. "We'll freeze!"

The conductor doesn't seem to hear her. "In an orderly fashion, please leave the train via the forward doors."

Grumbling, people start disentangling themselves from their seatbelts.

"This is ridiculous," Pigeon grumbles. "We should be going back to help that kid, not sitting around scratching our—"

"We can't go back until they're sure the train is safe," you say. "There was clearly something wrong with that kid's seatbelt, and the brakes took ages to slow us down. Who knows what else isn't working?"

Turn to page 59.

1 8:3 9

"**Y**ou're the one the security guard was looking for," you say.

Taylor looks uncomfortable. "I don't know what you're talking about."

"When I was getting on the train, a man asked me if I was Taylor. And he can't have been a friend of yours, since he clearly didn't know what you look like."

Taylor shrugs. "I haven't the foggiest idea who he was. So, which way shall we go? Up the mountain, or down?"

He's trying to change the subject. "Why would someone be looking for you?" you ask.

"I don't know, OK?" He throws his hands up in the air. "I just wanted to go snowboarding like a normal person. Was that too much to ask?"

"What do you mean, 'like a normal person?' Are you not normal?"

"Of course, I'm normal. It's my family that's—"

He stops talking abruptly. He looks a bit embarrassed, so you decide to go easy on him. After all, your family is kind of weird too.

When you look down, you see part of his seatbelt lying on the train tracks. The strap looks as if it has been cut with scissors.

"Someone sliced through your seatbelt," you say. "Deliberately."

He looks away.

"Is someone trying to . . . kill you?" you ask.

"No, no!" he says. "Nothing like that! Just . . . kidnap me, maybe."

"*Just kidnap* you?" You're starting to feel dizzy. "Who exactly is in your family?"

"No one."

You put your hands on your hips.

"Fine." He sighs. "I'll show you a picture of my third cousin twice removed."

"Your what?"

How would a photo of a distant relation help?

He pulls a dollar coin out of his pocket and shows you the design on one side.

It's a picture of Queen Elizabeth the Second.

"Are you telling me," you ask, "that the Queen of England is your *cousin*?"

"Third cousin," Taylor says. "Twice removed. I'm eighteenth in line for the throne."

You don't believe him, but he seems to *think* he's telling the truth. You rub your eyes. "I'm guessing you don't have a phone we could use to call for help?"

"No phone," Taylor says. "The servants usually make calls for me."

You groan. He believes he's royalty, and that falling

out of a moving train was fun. You're stuck out here in the wilderness with a crazy person.

Should you start walking down the mountain and try to get back to the station before you freeze to death? You can't see it through the falling snowflakes, but it can't be more than an hour away, and you won't get lost if you follow the tracks. Or should you wait here and hope the train comes back?

If you head back down the mountain, go to the next page.

If you stay where you are, go to page 25.

"OK, Your Majesty," you say. "Let's head back down the mountain to the station, where it's warm."

You trudge downhill, staying off the tracks in case the train comes back at high speed.

"I'm not actually a king, so 'Majesty' isn't appropriate," Taylor says pleasantly. "You should call me 'Your Grace.'"

You roll your eyes. "Sure thing, Your Grace."

"Now, if I were a prince, or — look out!"

Taylor grabs the hood of your jacket just in time. You jerk backward, away from the deadly ravine. The snowstorm is so thick you nearly stepped right into it. The walls are sheer and jagged rocks fill the valley below. Just the thought of falling in makes you feel sick.

"Thanks," you say, breathing heavily.

Taylor raises his thin eyebrows.

"Your Grace," you add.

He beams. "But of course. We can cross over there."

You walk on the train tracks to get over the ravine. The ground on the other side is lumpy beneath a thin crust of snow. You have to move carefully—a twisted ankle could leave you stranded up here. Taylor doesn't look strong enough to carry you.

He's still babbling about how cool it was, falling out the back of the train. He doesn't seem concerned about the kidnapping attempt. Maybe he really is royalty, and this happens all the time.

"Lucky I was wearing my ski gear," he says. "It's a bit chilly out here."

"Just a bit," you say, teeth chattering. "Also, if you weren't wearing it, the landing might have killed us both."

"All this *walking*," he says, ignoring you. "How much farther is the station?"

You shrug. "You don't like walking?"

"I usually have a driver. If I want to walk, I have to be surrounded by my security detail."

"Of course you do. Where was your security detail on the train?"

"One guard was seated next to me," Taylor says, "and the other was across the aisle."

"Uh-huh." You remember the man sitting next to Taylor, trying to grab him as he fell. Is it possible that he's telling the truth?

"Hey." Taylor stops walking. "Do you hear that?"

You listen to the distant hum. At first you think the train is coming back, but then you realize the sound is coming from farther down the mountain.

"A truck!" Taylor cries. "My uncle Myron is in

town—he must be here to rescue me!"

"Rescue *us*," you say.

"Quite." Taylor looks embarrassed. "That's what I meant."

The truck appears, driving up the train tracks toward you. It's a Hummer—a gigantic kind of four-wheel drive—painted white to match the snow.

They probably haven't seen the two of you yet. You grab Taylor's arm. "What if it's not your uncle? What if it's the people who tried to kidnap you?"

"Don't be ridiculous," Taylor says. "This is obviously him and his security escort."

If you trust Taylor and stay where you are, go to page 27.

If you drag him out of sight behind the nearest tree, go to page 29.

15:22

"We stay here," you say. "The train will be back any minute. If we head down the slope, we might freeze before they find us."

"We might freeze anyway," Taylor points out. "Not a lot of shelter out here."

You look around. He's right. The cold breeze sweeps down the barren mountain toward you. The bare trees shiver. Even the clouds look crystalline, like fairy floss.

"What did you say?" Taylor asks.

"I didn't say anything."

"You made a sort of growling noise."

You grit your teeth. "I didn't make any noise."

"Then what did?"

You look around at the rocks and snow. You can't see anyone or anything. What could live up here?

"Perhaps I imagined—" Taylor begins, but the sound interrupts him. This time you hear it too. *Rrrrrrrrrrr.*

"Maybe it's a lost dog," you suggest.

"There are no houses for miles. Who would lose their dog up here?"

"Maybe it's a sled dog that got loose."

The growling—or whatever it is—has stopped. The only sound left is the howling of the wind.

"It must be in there." Taylor points at some distant bushes clustered next to an outcropping of stone. "Nowhere else to hide. I'll check it out."

He tramps through the slush toward the outcrop.

"Are you crazy?" you demand. "Why would you go *toward* a growling wild dog?"

"I'm good with dogs," he calls back over his shoulder. "My third cousin keeps them."

"Those are *corgis*!" you shout, but he ignores you. You think about yelling some more, but you don't want to be too loud. The noise might trigger an avalanche.

If you follow Taylor to the bushes, go to page 52.

If you stay by the train tracks, go to page 75.

The Hummer slows down as it approaches you and Taylor. It rolls too close—so close you take a step back—before it stops.

After a pause, the passenger-side window rolls down. A head emerges. Tufts of gray hair stick out from under a brown golf cap. A small, carefully shaven chin jiggles. "Taylor, my boy! What are you doing out here?" Yet somehow the man looks only mildly surprised to see his nephew on the tracks.

"Uncle Myron!" Taylor cries, and sprints toward the Hummer.

You run after him, cursing yourself for being so paranoid. What if you had dragged Taylor into hiding? You might both have frozen to death. Still, something is bothering you, although you're not sure what.

"Get in here before you catch a cold!" Myron shouts. His head disappears and the window rolls up.

The door on the other side opens and the driver climbs out. He's a tower of muscle in a tight business suit. He has a brow like a caveman and ears that stick out.

"Hello, Derek," Taylor says.

The driver doesn't respond. He opens one of the rear doors and motions for the two of you to get in.

"Taylor," you say.

He pauses with one foot inside the Hummer. "What?"

"If they were trying to kidnap you, why would they sabotage your seatbelt? You could have died, and then there would be no ransom."

The driver's eyes narrow.

Taylor stares at you. "You're worried about how the kidnappers planned to make money? What is wrong with you?"

He clambers up into the Hummer. You follow him. The driver closes the door behind you.

The inside of the vehicle is divided into two sections, one for the driver and one for the passengers. A pane of tinted glass separates the two. The passenger compartment is luxurious, with leather upholstery and a little built-in fridge. A canvas backpack is stuffed under one of the seats, slightly unzipped. Through the gap you can see a phone.

Your phone is still broken, and you're not sure you trust "Uncle Myron." Maybe you should borrow this one—you could use it to call for help later.

Myron has chosen to ride up front with the driver. Neither is looking in your direction. Taylor is rummaging through the bottles in the mini-fridge.

Do you reach into the backpack and take the phone, or do you leave it? Make your choice, and turn to page 31.

Y ou haul Taylor into the prickly bushes surrounding a big tree nearby. He swears at you and tries to struggle free, but by the time he does, the vehicle has already swept past.

"Uncle Myron!" Taylor shouts, waving his arms. "Wait!"

The Hummer doesn't stop. It roars away up the hill, leaving you and Taylor alone in the freezing wind. There's another distant rumbling, like the one you heard at the station. The Hummer's engine, maybe?

"Fabulous," Taylor says. "What are we supposed to do now, genius?"

You're not sure. You didn't think this far ahead.

"We keep walking down the hill," you say. "Toward the station."

"And if we die of hypothermia before we get there?"

You say nothing. You've spotted an object half-buried in the snow. No, two objects; one of the wooden railway sleepers has split down the middle into two rough planks and been abandoned beside the tracks.

You pick the planks up. They're not especially heavy—years of rough weather have worn away much of the wood—but they still feel quite strong.

"I have an idea," you say. "Maybe we could—"

Another rumbling interrupts you. This time it gets louder and louder, shaking the earth beneath your feet.

"What is *that?*" Taylor shrieks.

BOOM! The mountain peak explodes behind you.

Rock and ash blast upward, turning the sky black. Chips of stone rain down. Mount Grave is a volcano!

"Run!" you yell, but Taylor is already sprinting down the hill. You dash after him. It's not cold anymore. A deadly heat is rising behind you. A river of melted snow trickles past. Your heart is pounding.

You could run faster if you dropped the two planks— but they might come in handy.

Do you keep the planks, or leave them behind? Make your choice and then turn to page 40.

A few seconds later, Taylor turns around with two bottles in his hands. "Would you care for some water," he asks, "or perhaps juice?"

"Thanks," you say. "Water, please."

He passes you the water bottle and settles back into his seat. He puts the seatbelt on very carefully, checking that the straps aren't damaged. You buckle up and sip your water. It's cold from the fridge—you wish there was something hot. Maybe there's a microwave somewhere in here? It doesn't seem unlikely.

The Hummer starts rumbling up the mountain again. The tires are so big that the ride doesn't feel bumpy, even though the vehicle is driving on train tracks.

"Why are we going up?" you ask. "Shouldn't we be heading back down to the station?"

Taylor looks at you like you're crazy. "My snowboard is on the train! We have to meet it at the top so I can get it and ride the slopes down."

"Haven't you had enough excitement for one day?" you ask.

He pumps his fist in the air. "Never!"

A royal adrenaline junkie. Now you've seen everything. You turn to the thick window. The Hummer is about to pass the gigantic ravine, which is much less scary from the safety of the car.

Taylor knocks on the glass that separates you from the driver's compartment. It buzzes as it rolls down.

"Everything OK, sport?" Uncle Myron asks.

"I was just wondering how far we were from the top," Taylor says.

"We'll be there soon, don't you worry."

"You must be wondering why we're not on board the train," you say.

Myron nods. "I was just about to ask."

"We fell out the back *while it was moving*!" Taylor says. "It was incredible."

"You should probably call someone at the station and tell them we're OK," you say.

"Oh, well, I already did," Myron says. "They were most relieved."

"But they didn't tell you what had happened?" you ask.

Myron changes the subject. "Are you kids warm enough back there?"

"Fine, thank you," Taylor says.

You have a very bad feeling about this. "Are you really royalty?"

"Indeed," Myron says. "Eighteenth in line for the throne."

"No, *I'm* eighteenth in line," Taylor objects. "You're nineteenth."

"Of course, of course," Myron says. But there's a dark sparkle in his eyes.

The Hummer slows to a halt beside the deadly ravine.

"Why are we stopping?" Taylor asks.

If you took the phone earlier, go to the next page.

If you didn't, go to page 36.

Keeping the phone hidden from Taylor, Myron, and the driver, you dial 911 and tuck it back into your pocket. Hopefully the call goes through, and the operator can trace it to your location.

Myron and the driver get out of the Hummer. The driver opens your door with one massive hand. Myron opens Taylor's.

"Don't do this," you say.

"Do what?" Myron asks. "I'm simply showing my nephew the amazing view."

Myron unbuckles Taylor's seatbelt and pulls him out of the car. The driver does the same to you.

You all stand there in the freezing cold on the edge of the ravine. Snowflakes tumble down, down, down into the darkness. Pigeon's voice echoes through your head. *The tallest mountain in the world . . . by how long it takes to hit the ground if you fall off the top.*

"Uh," Taylor says, "the view's great. Can we get back in the car?"

"Myron's going to throw you off!" you hiss. "So he'll be closer to becoming king!"

Taylor laughs. "Don't be silly."

Myron and the driver don't smile.

"That's a very serious accusation," Myron says.

"You got someone to sabotage Taylor's seatbelt," you say. "And since he survived that, you're going to push him over this cliff, to make it look like he died when he fell out of the train."

"You've gone mad!" Taylor tells you. "Right, Uncle Myron?"

Myron turns to the driver. "Push them both off."

The giant driver lunges at you. Taylor screams. The driver grabs your collar with one hand and Taylor's with the other. He drags you toward the cliff . . .

Turn to page 38.

03:40

"They're going to kill us!" you shout.

Taylor boggles at you. "Pardon?"

"What utter nonsense," Myron says, gray eyebrows rising.

"Don't you see? There was never any attempted kidnapping! *Myron* sabotaged your seatbelt. If you die, he's one step closer to the throne!"

"You're insane!" Taylor says. "Uncle Myron—"

But Myron is already raising the glass barrier back up. He and the driver step out of the Hummer and close the doors behind them.

All the locks click.

"Where are they going?" Taylor demands.

And then the Hummer starts rolling backward.

You unbuckle your seatbelt and wrench at the door handle, but it's locked. You're trapped!

"Myron!" Taylor yells. "We're stuck!"

The Hummer rolls faster and faster. You feel sick. You grab for the backpack, dig out the phone and dial emergency services—

But it's too late. The Hummer lurches backward, and suddenly you realize that it's falling over the cliff into the ravine!

"Noooooooo!" you scream, as the vehicle plummets down and down toward the jagged rocks . . .

THE END.

For another try, go back to page 22.

"I have your phone!" you scream.

Everyone freezes.

Myron looks faintly amused. "Pardon me?"

You dig the phone out of your pocket and hold it up. "I have your phone and I called 911 and they heard this whole conversation so you can't push us off the cliff because they'll know you did it," you say rapidly.

"Give me that!" Myron demands.

The driver grabs for the phone. You hold it out of reach.

"But," you say, "if you let us go, no one can prove that this wasn't all just a big joke."

Myron and the driver look at one another.

A distant thudding sound fills the air. You can see a helicopter circling overhead, searchlight beaming through the fog. The train conductor probably summoned it, but Myron doesn't know that. He might think it's the cops.

"Time to decide," you tell Myron. "Are you going to prison, or not?"

Myron glares at you for a long time.

"Let them go," he finally tells the driver.

"Yes, Your Grace." The driver releases your collar.

"I can't believe you would do this to me!" Taylor bellows at Myron.

"Do what?" Myron smiles. "This was all just a big joke."

00:00

You survived! There are ten other ways to escape the danger— try to find them all!

You catch up to Taylor quickly. He's sprinting down the tracks, screaming. He could probably run faster if he saved his breath, but you're too winded to tell him so.

It's hard to believe that only a minute ago you were worried about freezing to death. It's boiling now. You can feel the lava approaching. When you risk a glance over your shoulder, there it is in the distance: a bubbling river of orange rock streaming down Mount Grave toward you. Steam and ash blend to turn the air into a toxic fog.

"We're going to die!" Taylor wails. "We're going to die!"

"There!" you yell, pointing. Just off the tracks you can see a shadow in a rock wall. The closer you get, the surer you are—it's the entrance to a cave. Somewhere to shelter from the lava.

But as you run closer and closer, you start to worry. What if it's not deep enough? Or too deep—what if there's more lava inside? Maybe you should keep running down the tracks instead.

Taylor has seen the cave too. "Do we go in?" he shouts over the quaking of the mountain.

If you go into the cave, go to the next page.

If you keep sprinting down the slope, go to page 42.

You turn away from the rails and sprint toward the shadow, desperately hoping that it's a cave and not just a divot in the rock face. Taylor is right behind you, huffing and puffing. The heat of the lava singes your skin through your clothes.

You hit the shadow and keep going, sprinting into the pitch blackness of the cave. Yes! It's deep enough. Deep, and cool. There isn't any lava bubbling up within. Hopefully the flow outside will cruise right past.

You run through the darkness, arms outstretched until you crash into a wall. Taylor bumps into you.

"Keep going!" he hisses.

"I can't!" you say. "It's a dead end!"

The cave stops here. There's nowhere else to go.

"No!" Taylor cries. "The lava's right behind us!"

"What?" You look back, and then you see the tell-tale flickering glow. You can feel the heat. The lava is coming into the cave, as if it's hunting you.

"What do we do?" Taylor shrieks.

Earlier, did you pick up the two halves of the railway sleeper?
If you did, go to page 43.
If you didn't, go to page 44.

"**F**orget the cave!" you shout. "Keep running!"

You sprint desperately down the mountain, faster than ever before. Chunks of stone whistle past your ears like bullets. The lava hasn't reached you, but the rails are glowing red beneath your feet. It feels as though you are running on a hotplate.

You risk a glance over your shoulder. The top of the mountain is just gone, the remains of the shattered peak barely visible in the smoke. The lava is close, rolling down the hill toward you. But your real problem is the ash raining down from the sky like crows' feathers.

At school you learned about the ancient Roman town of Pompeii. When a volcano near Pompeii erupted, it wasn't the lava that killed everyone—it was the ash, burying eleven thousand people alive.

"I can't breathe!" Taylor cries. His face is black with soot. "We have to get out from under this ash cloud!"

Earlier, did you pick up the two halves of the railway sleeper?
If you did, go to page 45.
If you didn't, go to page 47.

The walls of the cave aren't smooth. There are cracks between the jutting rocks.

You toss one of the planks to Taylor. "Help me!"

"What are you doing?"

"Saving our lives."

You jam one end of the sleeper into a crack. Taylor gets the idea. He sticks the other plank into the crack and you both pull down with all your might.

The sleeper shifts the massive rocks. They tumble into the cave with a tremendous boom, blocking the path of the lava. When the echoes die away, you can't hear the eruption anymore. The rocks have blocked out all the sound from the outside world.

"At last," you say. "We're safe."

"Safe?" Taylor says. "We're trapped!"

Suddenly it dawns on you: he's right. The fallen stones may be keeping the lava out, but they're also keeping you in! You have no phone and no digging tools. The lava is already cooling, turning into solid rock.

You and Taylor are buried alive—forever!

THE END.

For another try, go back to page 29.

You don't have the planks, but the walls aren't sheer. You can see plenty of cracks to use as hand- and footholds.

"Climb!" you shout. "Go, go, go!"

Taylor scrambles up the wall like a possum up a tree. You follow him, fingers aching against the hot stone, the soles of your feet burning.

The ceiling isn't high. Soon you're both pressed up against it as the lava rolls into the cave beneath you.

"Now what?" Taylor demands.

"I don't know! I'm thinking."

But you're out of time. The air shimmers around you. It's too hot to breathe. You feel like you're a chicken roasting on a spit. And then a bubble pops in the lava below, shooting up a ball of fire—

THE END.

For another try, go back to page 29.

"Take this!" you shout, and throw one of the planks to Taylor.

He catches it. "What for?"

"Snowboarding!" Is it possible to use half a railway sleeper as a snowboard? You can only hope so.

"But there's no snow!" Taylor yells.

You look down. He's right. The snow has melted in the heat from the lava, leaving only a slushy mud made of water and ash.

"Ride the rails!" you cry. Without waiting for him to reply, you jump. In midair you press the plank to your feet and land sideways on one of the tracks. Suddenly you're sliding down the mountain like a pro skateboarder on a handrail.

Taylor gets the idea immediately. He leaps onto his plank with ease and zooms past you on the other rail, his arms stretched sideways for balance.

"Woohoo!" he bellows as he rockets away down the mountain.

You know how he feels. Despite the danger, it's thrilling; the wind blasting your face, the heat at your back, the pounding of your heart as you ride your improvised snowboard out of the ash cloud.

There's so much smoke in the air that it takes you a while to realize that some of it is coming from beneath you. When you look down, you realize that your plank is shooting sparks. The friction against the hot rails is burning through the wood.

"Taylor!" you shout. "My board's on fire!"

Go to page 48.

07:52

"Just keep running!" you scream, but you're not sure if Taylor hears you. The ash cloud descends thicker and thicker, clogging the air with black flakes. Even without carrying the added weight of the railway sleeper, you can't outrun it.

Taylor is invisible. The whole world has turned black.

"Taylor?" you yell.

No reply except the thundering of the mountain.

Now you're not so much running through the ash as swimming in it. The flakes sting your skin and burn the inside of your nostrils. You can't breathe. You can't breathe!

Your limbs go floppy and you slip off into a dreamless sleep, never to wake up.

THE END.

For another try, go back to page 29.

Taylor is too far ahead to hear. He's zooming down toward—

The train station. You're almost at the bottom of the mountain! There's blue sky above you; you're out of the ash cloud.

Something honks behind you. It sounds like the foghorn of a cruise ship. You look around and see the train careening down the mountain toward you.

They must have turned around when you and Taylor fell out the back. Now the train is traveling at top speed, trying to outrun the lava flow.

You throw yourself off the plank and land in the slush beside the tracks. You're out of harm's way, but that's not good enough. Your plank is lying sideways across the train's path. If the wheels hit it they could skip off the rails. Pigeon and everyone else on board is in danger.

You drag yourself back through the mud to the plank as the train thunders nearer. The churning of the gigantic wheels is deafening. They're too close. If you try to grab the plank, the rims could slice off your hand.

If you reach out and try to snatch the plank out of the way to save the train, go to the next page.

If you crawl to safety, go to page 51.

You grab the plank and pull. But it's jammed between the rails!

"No!" you scream, as the train thunders toward you.

You pull even harder, adrenaline filling your veins.

There! The plank comes free of the tracks. You tumble over backward just in time as the train rockets past, brakes shrieking. You scramble to your feet, coughing up soot, and chase it down the hill to the station.

Taylor has already climbed onto the platform by the time the train arrives. Two broad-shouldered men with crew cuts and black suits hustle out the doors of the train and huddle around him, as though he's the President of the United States and they're the Secret Service. One of them is muttering into his cufflinks, perhaps talking on a hidden radio.

They must be his security detail. He was telling the truth after all.

You haul yourself up onto the platform just as Pigeon walks out of the train.

"Pigeon!" you yell.

She turns around and gapes at you. Only then do you remember that you're covered in ash, mud, and splintered pieces of railway sleeper.

She hugs you anyway. "What happened to you?" she demands.

"I'll tell you on the way home," you say. "Let's get out of here. Next time, how about we go to the beach?"

00:00

You survived! There are ten other ways to escape the danger— try to find them all!

You dive backward just in time. The massive train wheels don't cut off your hand. But when they hit the plank, they skip off the rails and land in the mud.

The train stops dead and moans like a dying dragon as it starts to tilt, engine screaming, metal creaking, wheels churning against the ground. Too late, you realize that it's going to topple over—

And that it's going to land right on top of you!

You try to scramble out of the way, but the train is falling too fast. A hundred tons of steel block out the sun as the train tips over.

The last thing you see is Pigeon's terrified face behind the window.

Crunch!

THE END.

For another try, go back to page 29.

"Taylor! Wait up!" You follow him toward the bushes, trudging across the ice.

He's already touching the frost-rotted leaves and pulling them aside. "Here, puppy!" he says in a singsong voice. "Here, puppy! Here, pup!"

There's no dog. Instead, when he pushes the branches out of the way, a hole is revealed in the stone behind. It's a cave—no, wait, there are rails on the floor inside, and wooden support struts propping up the ceiling. It's a mine shaft. It must have been abandoned many years ago—long enough for these bushes to grow over the top of the entrance.

"Wow! Cool!" Taylor says.

You don't think it's cool. You think it looks like a great place to fall into a hidden pit and break your neck.

"Let's go in," Taylor says.

"Let's *not* go in," you say. "What if the train comes back and they don't see us?"

"What if we freeze to death before it gets here? We need to get out of this wind, at least for a while."

You stare into the gloom of the mine shaft. It doesn't exactly look warm, but you know Taylor's right. That wind is a killer.

"OK," you say finally. "But keep listening. We want to hear that train coming, all right?"

"Relax. They know where we fell off. They'll find us."

You're not convinced. Maybe you should scatter the broken pieces of your phone outside the cave entrance. They're shiny. They might be visible from the train window.

On the other hand, the fragments are also sharp. Someone might step on them and get hurt. But why would anyone be barefoot out here?

Do you fling the bits of phone out onto the snow, or do you leave them in your pocket? Make your choice, and then turn to page 56.

The conductor waits until everyone is seated before making an announcement over the PA: "OK, everybody, buckle up. We're going to head up to the top of Mount Grave so we can use the radio equipment to call for help."

You wonder if he came to this decision on his own or if you managed to convince him.

"Well," Pigeon says, "you got your way." She doesn't say *I hope you made the right decision,* but you can see her thinking it.

You don't reply. That's the trouble with unspoken criticisms; you can't respond to them.

"I'll ask you all to lean right back in your seats," the conductor says. "We'll be going at our top speed."

You press the back of your head to the seat just in time. The train launches forward like a ball out of a cannon. It's much faster than before—your whole body is crushed into the seat. There's a painful pressure in your head, as though your brain is being squished against the inside of your skull.

"Whooooooo!" Pigeon crows. At least she's having a good time. You turn your head to look at her, and immediately regret it. The force on your neck is enormous, and the trees are flying past the window so fast that you start to feel sick.

You're about to throw up all over Pigeon when the train begins to slow down. The wheels clatter with less and less vigor, and the squeezing inside your head fades. Is it possible that you're nearly at the top already?

The conductor seems to read your mind. "Welcome," he says, "to the peak of Mount Grave."

Go to page 130.

When you stoop to follow Taylor into the cave, you see him walking deeper into the darkness. "Where are you going?" you hiss.

"Why are you whispering?" he asks. "There's no one else around. That's our whole problem. *Helloooooo?*"

His voice bounces around the blackness of the mine shaft.

You shush him. "We should stay near the entrance."

"But look at this place!" He sweeps his arm around. "Why don't you want to explore?"

A growling echoes through the gloom, much louder than before. It sounds like an idling lawn mower.

"That's why!" you whisper.

All the color drains out of Taylor's face. "Where is that coming from?"

It's hard to tell. The dog—or whatever it is—could be deeper in the mine shaft. Or it could be concealed by the bushes just outside the entrance.

Which way should you go?

If you go farther into the tunnel, go to page 136.
If you head back toward the entrance, go to page 137.

As the bear pulls Taylor toward its terrifying maw, you run at it, waving your arms. "Let him go!" you scream.

There's no reason to believe that the bear speaks English, but the yelling actually seems to work. The creature gives you a puzzled look, and then drops Taylor. He hits the ground with a thump, whimpering.

"Now go away!" you shout.

The bear doesn't. Instead, it lumbers toward you, black lips peeling back over sharp teeth. Hot, foul breath washes over you.

"No!"

You turn to run, but it's too late. The bear grabs you, crushing your ankle with a mighty claw. You trip and land facedown in the dirt. Your nose stings as the bear drags you backward into the darkness of the mine shaft.

If you scattered the pieces of your phone outside the entrance, go to page 61.

If you didn't, go to page 63.

You sprint back toward the exit, leaving Taylor to his fate. His screams make you feel terrible—

But not for long. You hear a *thump*. When you turn to look, the bear has dropped Taylor. You distracted it by running, and now it's chasing after you!

You've been looking over your shoulder instead of watching where you were going. You trip over one of the mine-cart rails and slam hard into the floor, grazing your palms.

The *thud-thud, thud-thud* of the bear's paws echo around the tunnel as it catches up to you. You scramble to your feet just as the bear grabs your foot—

But it only gets your shoe. The claw leaves stinging gashes in your ankle as you slip free and dash toward the daylight, one foot bare. The bushes are just up ahead. After that you'll be out in the open.

If you scattered the pieces of your phone outside the entrance, go to page 64.

If you didn't, go to page 65.

19:09

You clamber off the train and find yourself standing in shallow snow beside the tracks. The wind has died down, and the silence is incredible. You never realized how noisy your home was—traffic noise, neighbors shouting, birds—until now.

Pigeon stamps her feet in the cold. "How long before we get moving again?"

"I don't know." You spot the conductor kneeling down beside the front of the train, fiddling with something underneath. "Let's go ask."

The conductor is muttering to himself when you approach. "Reservoir pipe—check. Secondary line—check. Control circuit—"

"Excuse me," you say.

He jolts and bumps his head on the underside of the car. "You kids should stay back," he says. "This engine might catch fire."

"Is that likely?"

"No," he admits. "What do you want?"

"We were just wondering when we would get moving again."

"Five minutes maybe. The question is, what direction will we take?"

"Won't we just head down the hill?" Pigeon demands. "To find that boy who fell out?"

"We could," the conductor says, "but he might be unconscious. We'd have to go very, very slowly or risk running over him. It might be quicker to go to the top of the mountain and radio for help. Then a four-wheel drive could go up from the bottom and find him."

He chews his lip. He looks sad—maybe disappointed that the maiden voyage is going so badly.

"Don't you have a radio on the train?" you ask.

"Only a short-range one," the conductor says, "and we're too high up to use it."

"I have a mobile phone," you offer. It's the only thing you brought, other than your compass.

He shakes his head. "The nearest transmission tower is on the opposite side of Mount Grave. By all means have a go, but at this height, the mountain almost always blocks the signal."

You take out your phone. Sure enough, the screen says *NO SIGNAL*.

Will you try to convince the conductor to go back down the hill, or to head for the top? Make your choice, and then go to page 132.

The bear hauls you deeper and deeper into its lair. You scrabble at the floor but there's no way to get free. The beast is too strong.

The mine shaft is full of old bones. A dog's rib cage here, a bird carcass there—and is that a human skull?

The bear stops. This must be the dining room. Holding you by the back of your shirt, the animal hauls you toward its jagged mouth. You scream as those yellow fangs come closer—

Zap!

The bear stiffens, eyes wide. Those massive claws clench you so tightly that it hurts. A crackling sound fills the air and the bear tilts over backward like a chair with a broken leg. It hits the ground with a mighty thud, trapping you under one of its forelegs.

What just happened? For a crazy second you think the bear is actually fake—a robot, and its software just crashed or something.

Then you hear voices.

"It's down, it's down."

"You got it?"

"I got it. Come on in."

Two security guards trudge into view. You recognize

one of them—the beak-nosed ticket checker from the train. She's holding a stun gun. She must have electrified the bear. If your feet had been touching the ground, you might have been shocked too.

"Wow," she says. "We should call the zoo. They'd probably love to get a specimen like this—hey! There's someone underneath!"

You try to call out, but the bear's leg has pushed all the air out of your lungs.

"Give me a hand!" The two security guards pull you out from under the stunned bear. "You OK, kid?" the woman asks.

You nod. "Thanks. Is Taylor all right?"

"That boy you were with? Yeah, he'll be fine. They're keeping him warm and giving him something to eat in the train."

"How did you find us?"

The woman frowns. "Funny thing. There was all this broken glass and plastic outside the entrance to the tunnel. A girl named Paige saw it from the train window."

You smile. It looks like you saved the day—with a little help from Pigeon.

00:00

You survived! There are ten other ways to escape the danger—try to find them all!

It's impossible to escape from the bear's mighty grip. No matter how much you struggle, it doesn't even seem to notice. The dirt scrapes your palms and your knees.

A foul stink fills the air. Worse than the bear's breath—it smells like rotten meat. The bear slows down, and you get a chance to peer around at the dim passageway. Dark splotches spatter the walls. The floor is littered with the remains of animals. Old bones. Things the bear has brought here to eat.

And now it's going to eat you!

"Noooo!"

You scream and belt at the bear's muscly hide. But it's useless. Under the matted fur it may as well be made of steel. The bear stretches open its terrifying jaws and hauls you in, head first.

Crunch!

THE END.

To try again, go back to page 52.

You claw your way through the bushes. Part of you is hoping the train will be waiting right outside and you can hide on board. Could the bear tear open the train?

It doesn't matter. When you emerge from the bushes, the train isn't there. Just snow and rocks and empty rails on the mountain slope.

The bear is right behind you. You sprint away from the mine shaft as fast as you can—

But a piece of your broken phone gets stuck in the sole of your bare foot.

"Ow!" You stumble and fall, hitting the snow face first. How could you have forgotten about the phone?

The bear roars. Your eardrums throb under the strain. You roll over just in time to see the beast pounce like a gigantic dog. It hangs in the air above you for a split second, blocking out the sun, about to crush you with its weight.

You don't even have time to scream.

Wham!

THE END.

To try again, go back to page 52.

You haul yourself through the bushes, twigs scratching your arms and your bare foot, before you stumble out into the snow. You had hoped the bear would be reluctant to leave its cave, but you can hear it snuffling and grunting behind you. It isn't going to give up the chase.

You dash across the snow toward the train tracks. A small pile of stones is on the other side. If you can get to them, maybe you can defend yourself.

Usually it would be a very bad idea to throw rocks at a bear. But it's angry at you anyway—you figure things can't get much worse.

You run across the tracks to the rock pile. But when you're almost there your bare foot sinks into a hole hidden under the snow.

"Argh!" You flop forward onto the ground. Pain shoots up your shin. When you roll over, you see the bear crossing the tracks toward you, a hungry grin on its shaggy face—

Wham!

The train car seems to come out of nowhere, slamming into the bear and sending it flying. The emergency brakes wail and the train stops almost immediately, perhaps because it wasn't going very fast, or perhaps because the bear absorbed most of its momentum. The bear hits the ground with a thump and makes a baffled groan.

The doors pop open. Pigeon jumps out and runs over to you. "You're alive!"

"My leg hurts," you grumble. But she's right. You *are* alive—you survived falling out of a train *and* getting attacked by a bear, all in the space of thirty minutes.

In the distance, Taylor is limping out of the mine shaft. "You saved my life!" he shouts. You wonder if he knows you did it by accident.

A security guard gets off the train, talking into a radio. "Yep, found them both. But we'll need a doctor," she says, looking at your leg.

The bear groans again.

"And a vet," the guard adds.

00:00

You survived! There are ten other ways to escape the danger— try to find them all!

03:10

You sling the belt outwards. It scrapes along the side of the train and—

Yes! It catches on the edge of the running board, just below the doors.

You barely have time to congratulate yourself before the train wrenches you off your feet. You cling desperately to the belt as the train drags you down the slope behind it. A freezing wind blasts your face. Your flailing legs leave twin trails through the snow. Ice fills up your shoes and your fallen pants, both of which eventually tear off. Your bare feet turn blue in a matter of seconds.

But it's working. The train accelerates while the avalanche slows down and dies out. Soon you've left the deadly wall of sliding ice behind.

But more danger lurks ahead. The rails are about to leave the snowy part of the mountain and speed onto the rocky plains. When the train gets there, you won't be able to keep skating alongside it. Your legs will break on the stone.

The train's brakes shriek. Someone must have seen you clinging to the side. But it's not going to stop in time to save you.

You let go of the belt. The train flings you clear like

a bull throwing off a rider, and you slam into a nearby snowdrift. The powder isn't as soft as it looks—the impact jars every joint and ligament in your body.

But you can lift your head. Your spine is OK.

The train squeals to a stop over the rocks. The doors hiss open and someone sprints back toward you.

It's Pigeon.

"Hey!" she screams. "Are you all right?"

You roll over and groan. "I'm OK. Taylor, the other kid—he's in a cave up the hill. Someone should go get him."

Pigeon helps you to your feet. "We'll find him, don't worry." She beckons over some of the other passengers, who are stumbling out of the train in a daze.

You take a deep breath. You can't believe you survived.

"I have to ask," Pigeon says, "where are your pants?"

00:00

You survived! There are ten other ways to escape the danger—try to find them all!

"OK," the conductor says, when everyone is seated. "I've inspected the train, and everything seems to be in good shape. We're going to head back down the hill nice and slow and try to find our missing passenger. I'd appreciate it if you all took a look out the windows for signs of him."

The train starts sliding down the mountain. It's alarming to roll backward on such a steep slope, but at least the conductor did what you said.

Pigeon buckles herself in. "I'm glad we're going back," she says, "but it's a shame we won't get to see the top of the mountain."

"Maybe we will," you say. "One time I went to the movies and the projector broke down, so they gave us free tickets for another session."

"You'd take this train a second time? If they give me a free ticket, I'm selling it online."

You shrug and look out the window, searching for the lost passenger. A noise is getting louder. It takes you a moment to recognize it—the helicopter has come back.

You search the sky out the window. You can't see it, but it must be close. The sound of the blades is making the walls shudder.

"Bandits!" the conductor yells. "Everyone fasten your seatbelts."

The train accelerates down the mountain. It feels like being in an elevator that is descending too fast.

"What's going on?" Pigeon demands. "I thought he said we had to go slow?"

"It's like he's trying to outrun the helicopter," you say.

"Why? What does he—"

Something crashes down on the roof. The ceiling buckles inward. The lights fizzle out. The train fills with screams as it rocks from side to side.

The helicopter has landed on top of the train!

The window next to Pigeon explodes, showering you both with tiny cubes of plastic you thought were shatterproof. At the same moment a window bursts on the opposite side of the train. Grappling hooks shoot through the gaps and latch onto the frame.

"What's going on?" Pigeon shrieks.

"They're attaching the helicopter to the train," you shout. "So we can't shake it off."

"But who are they?"

If you move away from the windows as fast as possible, go to page 78.

If you stay where you are and try to dislodge the grappling hook, go to page 81.

You dash down the mountain as the avalanche gains momentum behind you. But it's hard to run downhill at the best of times, and the ground is shaking. Your shoes keep slipping on the jolting, shuddering rocks.

You turn your head to look at the approaching wall of ice. It's catching up, and it's not just snow. It's a growing tidal wave of stones and trees, crashing down the slope toward you—

And the train!

The train is hurtling down the rails just ahead of the avalanche, like a surfer riding a breaking wave. The engine screams. It must be going at top speed.

You can't outrun the avalanche, but maybe the bullet train can.

You swerve sideways, sprinting toward the tracks.

"Hey!" you yell, waving your arms. "Slow down!"

It doesn't. And you can't get on board while the train is moving. But maybe there's another way to get to safety.

As you run, you unbuckle your belt and wrench it out of your trousers. They start to fall down almost immediately, leaving you shuffling like a manacled prison inmate, but you're almost at the tracks. The train is bearing down on you, the wall of snow right behind it.

You grab both ends of the belt in one hand, bending it into a loop. You fling the belt toward the train, hoping to snag something, anything.

It's a fifty-fifty shot.

Go to page 80 . . .

or to page 67.

The cascading ice roars closer and closer. You dash after Taylor into the darkness of the cave, just in time—the snow smashes down behind you, piling up and up outside the entrance. Had you hesitated just a second longer you would have been crushed.

"Are you OK?" you ask.

"Fine." Taylor is breathing heavily. "You?"

You nod. "But we're trapped!"

"No." Taylor points. "Look."

The snow hasn't completely blocked the entrance to the cave—the sky is visible through a little gap at the top. The wind whistles through the hole.

You're not going to suffocate. You might even be able to dig your way out. You pick up a rock, ready to start breaking through the snow.

"Ouch!"

Something bites the back of your hand. You look down and see a spider scuttling up your wrist, just like the ones on Taylor's face.

But on closer inspection, it's not a spider at all.

It's a huge tick!

You slap at it, and miss. It disappears into your sleeve.

"Taylor!" you cry. "There's a—ow!"

Another bite, this time on your leg. You look down in time to see two more ticks crawl over your boots and up your trouser legs.

"Help me!" you scream. But the words don't come out properly. Your swollen tongue gets in the way.

Taylor is scratching himself all over, as though he's covered in itching powder. Bloated red lumps are growing on his face.

The ticks bite your thighs, your belly, your neck. You can feel their tiny claws all over you.

You run over to the wall of ice and start hacking away at it with the rock, but it soon slips out of your fingers. Your hand has gone purple and inflated to twice its normal size.

"Mmmnff!" you mumble. Your vision blurs. Your legs slide out from underneath you. You barely feel yourself hitting the ground.

Your last thought is of Pigeon. She would be so jealous if she knew you had found the legendary ticks.

THE END.

For another try, go back to page 25.

ou hover by the train tracks as Taylor disappears into the bushes. Soon the leaves stop jiggling and the echoes of his footsteps fade away, leaving you completely alone. It's as if he never existed.

You look up the mountain. No sign of the train. When you turn the other way, you can't see anyone coming from the bottom of the mountain either.

Is this how you die? Not in a car accident, not in a hospital bed, but on a frozen slope, waiting for the Queen's third cousin to come back while your blood slowly turns to ice?

Taylor has been gone a long time now. Maybe the growling thing has eaten him. But surely that would have been noisy? There's been nothing but silence from the bushes since he disappeared.

"Taylor?" you call out.

Your voice bounces off the distant rocks, coming back again and again, quieter each time.

There is no response.

You step away from the tracks and start walking toward the bushes. Taylor might need your help. He might have tripped and knocked himself out. You can't just leave him.

As you get closer to the bushes, you think you hear a noise. It sounds like someone—or something—breathing heavily.

"Taylor?" you say again.

No reply.

Heart pounding, you reach out and peel the bushes aside—

Revealing a cave. The entrance is so narrow that the bushes concealed it almost completely.

The breathing sound stops.

"Hello?" you call.

Something shifts in the darkness, and then—

"Boo!" Taylor leaps out of the cave, waving his arms.

You scream. Not just because he startled you, but because spiders are crawling all over his face.

"You're covered in spiders!" you shriek.

"What? Argh!" Taylor bats at his arms and legs, squashing the scuttling creatures. He hops from foot to foot as though standing on hot coals.

"Your face!" you yell. "They're on your face!"

He screams and starts slapping his cheeks and forehead. Spiders explode into globs of yellow goo.

Soon all the spiders are squished, and you've both stopped screaming. The echoes die away—

To be replaced by a dark rumbling sound, just like the one you heard at the station.

"What is *that*?" Taylor hisses.

It's not until you see the foaming whiteness at the top of the mountain, like the crest of a breaking wave, that you figure it out.

"Avalanche!" you cry.

The wall of sliding snow approaches. Taylor bolts back into the cave. You could follow him, but what if the entrance filled up with snow? You'd never be able to dig your way out. And what about the spiders?

Perhaps you should sprint downhill instead. But can you really outrun an avalanche?

If you go into the cave, turn to page 73.

If you run down the mountain, go to page 71.

"**G**et away from the windows!" you shout.

You and Pigeon jump back just in time. Two men swoop in, one through each of the empty window frames, boots first. They land on the broken pieces of window inside the train car, one brandishing a scratched-up sword, the other wielding a lumpy club. Pale scars lattice their skin.

"Listen up!" the bandit with the sword bellows. He has about half as many teeth as he should have. "Do exactly as we say and nobody gets hurt."

The man with the club raises it menacingly. You step back and put your hands in the air. Other passengers are already scrambling toward the rear of the train, away from the two bandits.

"Drop it," the guy with the sword says.

You turn to see the beak-nosed security guard holding up a stun gun. She lets it fall to the floor.

"Good." The bandit lowers his sword and turns to face the rest of the group. He has massive forearms and a neck thicker than his head. "I want you all to take out your mobile phones and hold them in the air," he says. "Slowly."

The other passengers rifle through their pockets and

hold up their phones. The bandit with the club walks around, snatching phones out of hands and dropping them into a canvas bag.

If you can keep your phone hidden, maybe you can call the police. Perhaps the bandit will believe that a kid your age might not have a phone.

If you hold up your phone, go to page 90.

If you pretend you don't have one, go to page 92.

The belt smacks against the side of the train—
And catches nothing. It bounces off.

"No!" you cry.

The train rockets away down the slope, leaving you staring helplessly after it, your trousers around your ankles—

And then the wall of snow slams into you from behind.

It happens so fast, with such force, that you don't even have time to scream before the whole world goes black.

THE END.

For another try, go back to page 75.

You lunge toward the empty window frame, reaching for the grappling hook. Hopefully you can dislodge it from the train car.

"Pigeon!" you yell. "Get the other one!"

Pigeon runs to the hook on the other side of the train while you fiddle with this one.

Yes! The hook comes loose from the window frame—

But then the cable goes taut, pulling you out the window with it!

You tumble out into the daylight, clinging desperately to the hook as the ground rushes by below you. The helicopter looms above, perched atop the train like a gigantic mosquito. The parts are dirty and mismatched, as though it was pieced together from several different vehicles. The whirling blades are deafening. They seem to be accelerating rather than slowing down.

The helicopter is taking off again!

The plan must have been to lift the train off the tracks so it could be disassembled and sold. But that won't work, because you detached the grappling hook. On the other side of the train, the second hook swings loose—Pigeon must have gotten to it in time. You hope she won't get pulled out the window like you did.

The helicopter rises, taking you with it. Your feet kick uselessly in the air. The ground below gets farther and farther away.

The chopper tilts forward to chase the escaping train. You swing sideways on the rope, now about thirty feet above the snow.

A row of spiky trees looms ahead. It looks like the helicopter is going to fly over them, dragging you into the maze of pointed branches and lethal trunks.

You could let go of the hook, but landing on the snow from such a height might break your legs. Or you could climb up the rope toward the helicopter to avoid hitting the trees, but that would leave you even higher above the ground.

What do you do?

If you crawl up the rope, go to page 84.

If you drop to the ground, go to the next page.

You let go of the rope. It slips through your fingers and you fall—

But only two feet. The hook snags the hood of your coat, stopping you from falling any farther. The zipper jerks upward, pressing hard against your throat.

You choke, arms flailing as you try to grab the rope. Maybe you can pull yourself back up and take the pressure off your neck.

But it's no use. The grappling hook is behind your head, and reaching for it just makes you spin around. First, you're facing the mountain, then the train tracks, and then—

The trees, which are rushing toward you, reaching out with deadly branches.

You could try to slip out of your coat and drop to the ground. But it's a long way down now, and the ice below looks flat and hard. Maybe you should grab hold of the approaching trees instead.

If you slip out of the coat, go to page 138.
If you try to grab the trees, go to page 139.

You scramble up the rope as the helicopter flies closer and closer to the trees.

Are you going to make it?

You're just in time. The first tree scrapes the sole of your shoe as you fly over it. But some of the other trees are taller, with longer, sharper branches. You climb higher still, heart pounding.

What will happen when the helicopter catches up to the train again? The bandits will probably reel in the hooks so they can try to reattach the chopper to the train.

And you'll get reeled in too. You'll be trapped in a helicopter full of bandits. You picture them—sneering faces and foul breath, waving swords or guns. What will they do? Just throw you overboard?

You're trying to come up with a new plan when the helicopter stops dead in the air. The rope goes suddenly taut, almost throwing you off. When you look down, you see that the grappling hook is tangled in one of the trees. The helicopter has accidentally tethered itself like a hot air balloon.

Beyond the trees, the train is zooming away down the mountain at a breakneck pace.

You shimmy down the rope into the trees, ignoring

the scratches on your hands as you grab the branches.

The rope quivers. You look up, squinting against the blinding sun, and see a bandit leaning out of the helicopter. His dusty overcoat billows in the wind as he searches for the source of the problem.

He sees you, perched in the tree like a lost cat.

His eyes narrow. He draws a dagger, clenches it between his teeth like a pirate, and starts to climb down the rope toward you.

At first you think he's just going to cut through the rope so the helicopter can fly away. But if that was his plan, he would have cut it from the top. Instead he's climbing down to retrieve the grappling hook.

Which means the knife is meant for you.

You look around. But the train is long gone, and no one else is in sight. No help is coming.

You dig through your pockets. Maybe you can cut the rope so he can't get to you. But all you have is your phone, your compass, and your train ticket.

The edge of the compass is sort of sharp. Perhaps it could slice through the rope?

If you climb down the tree to escape, go to page 88.

If you try to hack through the rope with the sort-of sharp edge of your compass, go to the next page.

You press your compass against the rope and start sawing at the fibers. The outer layer gets shredded surprisingly quickly. Encouraged, you cut faster.

But then disaster strikes. You're only about a quarter of the way through when the sound changes, like plastic on metal. You peer at the scrape marks. It looks like the rope has a tightly wound steel core, designed to stop it from fraying or snapping. You hack at it with more force, but it just wears away the edge of your compass.

You look up. The bandit is nearly upon you, although it's hard to see him through the smoke.

Smoke?

Suddenly you feel the heat and see what you've done. The compass has a magnifying glass built into it, and it's concentrating the sun's rays onto one of the branches. The branch has started to smolder, and little wisps of flame have spread to the withered leaves.

You blow gently on the fire, encouraging it.

The bandit scrambles back up to the helicopter as the fire spreads. You climb down the tree toward the ground, trying to outrun the flames.

A charred branch snaps, showering you with hot sparks and freeing the grappling hook. The helicopter lurches away into the smoky sky, the bandit clinging to the underside. Hopefully the train has reached the bottom of the mountain where the police are close, so the bandits won't attack again.

You drop from one bough to the next, eyelids almost shut to ward off sparks and scraping branches. Soon you're only six feet above the ground and you jump, crashing down onto the snow and stumbling away from the burning tree.

Except it's not burning anymore. The branches are still smoking, but the trunk itself must be too wet and cold to burn. None of the other trees around it have caught fire.

You survived the helicopter, the bandit, and the fire. You lie on your back in the snow, watching clouds of mist appear above your head as you exhale.

It's a long walk down the mountain. You'll need your strength.

00:00

You survived! There are ten other ways to escape the danger—try to find them all!

You clamber down the tree like a monkey trying to escape from a puma. The branches leave red scratches all over your hands.

The bandit reaches the bottom of the cable and starts climbing through the leaves toward you. He's catching up fast.

You're at a disadvantage. The bandit wears protective clothes under his coat, so he doesn't have to worry about getting gutted by a sharp twig. You, meanwhile, are dressed for a nice comfortable train ride, not a deadly chase through the forest.

But if you can get to the ground before he does, you can sprint away into a thicker cluster of trees. The helicopter won't be able to spot you from above, and the bandit is bigger than you, so maybe you can squeeze through gaps where he won't fit.

You're almost at ground level. You let go of the last branch and fall toward the snow—

But something grabs you from above.

"OK!" the bandit yells. "Pull us up!"

A radio crackles. *"Pulling."*

You scream as you're dragged back up into the trees by your collar. The bandit holds you with one hand

and the rope with the other as the helicopter ascends, hauling you both up out of the forest and into the air.

The rope retracts, carrying you higher and higher until you're both hanging right beneath the chopper, hundreds of feet above the ground. You stop struggling. If he loses his grip, you're dead.

A woman leans out the open door of the helicopter. "Any luck?"

"Train's long gone," the bandit says. This close, he smells terrible. "But we have a new recruit."

He lifts you up with one mighty arm and hurls you into the helicopter. You slam down onto the metal floor, which is slippery with engine grease.

The woman stands over you, a wrench in one hand. Her hair looks like it was cut with a knife.

"You'll work twelve hours a day, seven days a week," she tells you, "but you'll get an equal share of everything we take. What do you say?"

She extends a grimy hand.

If you accept the bandits' offer, go to page 134.
If you refuse, go to page 135.

You hold your phone in the air. The bandit snatches it out of your hand and throws it into the bag. You wonder if you've made a mistake.

The other bandit, the one with the sword, is kicking the door to the conductor's cabin. On his third kick, the hinges crack. He rips the door out of the frame and drags the terrified conductor into the car.

"All right," the bandit with the club yells. "Listen up. In one minute this train will depart for the top of the mountain."

Sword Bandit sits down in the conductor's chair and starts fiddling with the controls. The engine rumbles.

"But if I were you," Club Bandit continues, "I would get off here."

He slaps the button for the rear door, which slides open, revealing the frosty mountainside. The train starts to move slowly up the hill.

You sigh. It feels like you've spent all day getting on and off this stupid train.

"Come on, get a move on." Club Bandit grabs someone and throws them out onto the tracks. You and Pigeon are near the back of the crowd. By the time it's your turn to jump off, the train might be going quite fast.

It doesn't look like the bandits have done a head-count. Maybe you should just hide under one of the seats. But what will you do when the train reaches the top of the mountain?

If you jump off the moving train, go to page 101.

If you hide, go to page 103.

You reach into your pocket and punch in 911. Then you hold both hands up, empty, leaving your phone nestled snugly in your pocket.

"What are you doing?" Pigeon whispers.

You shush her. Hopefully the call will go through and the police will hear what's going on and be able to trace the call.

The lanky man in the broad-brimmed hat hasn't raised his hands. "I don't have a phone," he says, when the bandit with the bag approaches him.

"I'll give you five seconds to reconsider that answer," the bandit says.

"It's broken," the man says. "I left it at home."

The bandit raises the club. "Five. Four. Three. Two—"

"OK, OK!" the man cries. "Take it!" He digs through his pockets, rips out a phone, and hands it over.

The bandit puts it in the bag without even looking at it. "Smart decision."

You're not feeling so good about your choice. But it's too late to change your strategy—or is it?

You reach into your pocket and pull out your compass. It's black and rectangular, with glass bits. It might be mistaken for a phone, if the bandit isn't looking drops her phone into the bag, the bandit.

You're next in line. You hand the compass to the bandit.

He takes it and puts it in the bag.

Then he does a double-take and pulls it back out again.

"What's this?" he demands.

You roll your eyes, as if that's the dumbest question you've ever heard. "It's a compass phone? Duh."

The guy turns it over, examining it from all sides. Your heart is pounding.

"Here," you say, holding out your hand. "I'll show you how to make calls on it—"

The bandit bats your hand away. "Nice try," he sneers, and drops the compass into his bag.

You breathe out as he walks away. Pigeon stares at you as if you've just revealed that you're a Jedi.

"Take this," you murmur, and slip the phone into her hand. "They might wise up and search me later."

Pigeon nods and slides the phone into her pocket.

The other bandit is at the front of the train, banging on the door to the conductor's compartment.

"Open up!" he roars.

The conductor doesn't respond.

"I know you're in there," the bandit shouts. He kicks

steel-capped boot. The hinges rattle. ...

...ore kicks and he'll probably get through.

...at will he do to the conductor?

...he sword glints in the bandit's hand.

If you talk to the bandit and try to stall him, go to the next page.

If you stay back, go to page 97.

"Wait," you shout, walking toward the bandit. "I know how to get in."

The bandit turns to face you. He points the sword at you. The sharp tip is only inches from your throat.

"How?" he asks.

"There's a switch," you lie. "For emergencies. Just promise you won't hurt anybody."

"Show me."

You reach past him and knock on the door. "I'm going to tell him where the emergency switch is," you yell. "So you may as well just open the door."

There's no response from the conductor, just as you hoped.

"I'm going to give you one minute," you shout. "Sixty. Fifty-nine. Fifty-eight—"

The bandit grabs your shoulder. "Forget that," he says. "Just show me where the switch is."

"OK," you say. You lead him down the stairs to the far end of the train. The crowd parts to let you through.

"Why would the switch be up this end?" the bandit asks, starting to get suspicious.

"It's not," you say. "It's near the front, but it's on the outside."

You hit the button by the train door. The rear door slides open, exposing the snowy mountain-scape. The wind wails at you.

"If it's out there, how do you know about it?"

The lie comes easily. "We had to stop for a safety check. I saw the switch when the conductor was fiddling with the brakes. Come on."

You step out and climb down onto the snow. The bandit follows.

Turn to page 99.

The bandit with the sword thumps on the door again. "OK, listen up," he yells. "Are you listening?"

No response from the conductor. You have the sudden feeling that he's not even in there—that he escaped out an emergency exit and is running away through the snow outside.

Or maybe he's hurt. The train stopped very suddenly—he could have bumped his head. He might be lying on the floor inside, unconscious.

"I'm going to give you five seconds to open the door," Sword Bandit continues. These guys seem to be big fans of the "five second" method. "If you don't open it, one of these passengers gets a cracked skull."

You don't sense Club Bandit sneaking up behind you until it's too late. He grabs your shoulder so you can't run away.

"Five," Sword Bandit says.

"No!" Pigeon cries.

"Four."

"Don't do this," you stammer.

"Three."

"The conductor might not even be in there!"

"Two."

The bandit raises the club high above your head.

"Or he might be hurt," you say, "knocked out. Please, don't—"

"One."

The club comes crashing down, and the whole world goes dark.

THE END.

For another try, go back to page 78.

The air chills you all the way down to your bones. You and the bandit with the sword tramp through the slush toward the front of the train.

The bandit shoves your back. "Hurry up," he says.

"I can't go any faster," you say. "I hurt my knees skateboarding."

"I don't care. Keep moving."

When you reach the front, you crouch down and peer under the train. You can't see the switch—and then you remember that you made it up.

You stick your hand into the darkness in front of the massive wheels. "I can't reach it," you say.

You expect the bandit to get down on his hands and knees to take a look, but he doesn't. Instead he just waggles the sword at you.

"Crawl under there and flip it," he snarls.

You wriggle into the space under the train. You can see plenty of pipes and bolts, but nothing that looks plausibly like a switch.

"It's stuck," you say.

"Then push harder!" the bandit shouts. "Or I'll cut your feet off."

Your breathing quickens in the darkness. "I'm trying!"

You can hear the blade tapping against the side of the train. "I'm warning you," the bandit says. "If you don't—hey!"

"You're under arrest," another voice says. You can hear the sound of handcuffs ratcheting closed.

"I'll kill you!" the bandit yells.

"Add 'threatening a police officer' to the list of charges, will you, Jenkins?" the voice says.

A friendly face appears beneath the train. Brown eyes focus on you.

"You can come out now," the police officer says.

You crawl out. "How did you get here so fast?"

"There's a kid down at the bottom of the mountain. He says he fell out the back of the train, hiked down the tracks, and called us when he saw the helicopter land on the train."

So if you had saved the boy from falling out of the train, he wouldn't have been able to call for help, and you might both be dead right now. It's almost too much to wrap your head around.

The cop helps you to your feet. "It's OK," he says. "You're safe."

00:00

You survived! There are ten other ways to escape the danger— try to find them all!

By the time you and Pigeon get to the front of the line, the train is moving dangerously quickly. If you jump out, won't you break your legs?

"Quick," Pigeon says. "Before it gets any faster."

She hurls herself out the train door, landing like a cat between the rails. She turns around immediately and starts running after the train. "Jump!" she yells at you. "Come on!"

You stare down at the rushing blur of railway sleepers. The open door seems to suck all the air out of the train. You can feel Club Bandit looming behind you. Your heart is pounding.

You crouch down.

"Too slow," Club Bandit says, and pushes you out the door.

You scream as you tumble out into the daylight and crash down into the snow.

Pain flares up all over your body. You lie still on the tracks, too dizzy to stand, listening to the train clatter away up the mountain.

Footsteps crunch toward you. You turn your head to see Pigeon running over.

"Hey," she says. "Are you OK?"

You cough and give her a thumbs up. The bandits won—but at least you're alive.

00:00

You survived! There are ten other ways to escape the danger— try to find them all!

"I'm staying," you whisper to Pigeon. Her eyes widen. You check that neither bandit is looking at you. Then you squeeze yourself into the space under one of the chairs. Pigeon does the same.

"What will we do when we get to the top?" she murmurs.

"Escape while their backs are turned," you say. "Try to get to the station and call for help."

"But what if they find us?"

You're worried about the same thing. "They won't," you say.

The other passengers have all jumped off.

"Huh," one of the bandits says. "That went well."

"Easier than I expected," the other bandit says. His voice is higher now, as if he was intentionally putting on a tough-guy sound before. "Come on."

Their boots clomp up the stairs toward where you and Pigeon are hiding. You hold your breath and squeeze your eyes shut, as though they won't be able to see you if you can't see them.

The bandits walk past without slowing down.

You open your eyes. Pigeon has an amazed grin on her face. You wink at her.

"Top Shelf, do you read me? Over."

A radio squawks and bleeps. *"This is Top Shelf. What is your status?"*

"The train is clear. We'll be in position soon. Get the chopper ready."

You give Pigeon a thumbs up. It sounds like the bandits are going to ride their helicopter out of here as soon as they've moved the train to a safe place. Once they're gone, you and Pigeon can escape—and you can reveal the location of the stolen train to the police. You'll be heroes.

But something is bothering you. How will the bandits hide the train? They can't get it off the rails, can they?

The train's brakes squeal. The seats shudder as the wheels slow down.

"OK," one of the bandits says. "We're in position."

"Locking on now."

You hear something clank beneath the floor, like a clamp pinning the wheels in place. The train stops abruptly.

The doors hiss. The two bandits walk off the train. Just as the doors close, you hear Club Bandit say one last thing into the radio: "Activate the chopper."

"OK," you whisper to Pigeon. "We'll wait until we hear the helicopter take off, and then we'll run."

"Good plan. Do you think—"

Pigeon doesn't get any farther. An enormous blade

smashes down through the train, neatly slicing the driver's compartment away from the rest of the car. It's as if a giant is attacking the train with a meat cleaver.

The blade rises back up out of sight.

You scream and flee toward the other end of the train, just in time. The tremendous blade crashes down again, ripping the seats in half as it shears off another segment of the train. The chopper isn't a helicopter. It's a machine designed to chop up the train!

Pigeon is already at the back door of the train. "It won't open!" she shrieks.

You slam your hand on the emergency button. She's right. The two of you are trapped, and the blade is getting closer every second.

"We'll have to jump out!" you yell.

"But the door won't open!"

"Not that way." You point to the other end of the car, where the blade is carving through the metal like an axe through a sponge cake. "That way."

"We'll be turned into mincemeat!" Pigeon shouts.

"It's our only shot."

You watch the blade get closer and closer as it chops off more and more of the car. It rises up, clearing the way for you. You'll have to time this perfectly.

If you jump out, go to page 129.

If you tell Pigeon to go first, go to page 12.

"Good thinking," you say, and follow Pigeon around the corner. The view isn't as good from this side, but at least your skin isn't crystalizing.

A little window is protected by wrought-iron bars. Through it you can see the conductor's bald patch as he talks rapidly into an old-fashioned telephone.

"So," Pigeon says, "quite a day we've had."

"It's not over yet," you say. You're trying to be optimistic, but the words come out sounding ominous.

"I don't understand," the conductor is saying. "What are you talking about?"

You lean closer to the window so you can hear him better.

"What are you doing?" Pigeon asks. You shush her.

"Listen to me," the conductor continues. "There's a boy stranded halfway up the mountain. He fell out of the train. He's probably badly injured. You need to send someone right away."

There's a pause. You can hear the muffled mumbling of whoever is on the other end of the line.

"What does it matter how many people are with me?" the conductor demands. "I'm telling you—"

Movement catches your eye. You turn just in time to

see the man in a ski mask duck out of sight below the edge of the platform.

"Did you see that?" you ask Pigeon.

"See what?"

More movement, on the other side of the platform this time, near the huddled crowd of passengers. You whirl around. Another man in white camouflage gear is lurking behind the broken vending machine.

"We're in trouble," you say. "Two guys—"

Someone grabs you by the hair.

Pigeon screams. You can't turn your head to see who's holding you, but you can see that you're not the only one who has been attacked. Yells ripple out from the passengers as three more camouflaged men materialize among them, grabbing their arms and shoulders.

The guy with the camera shouts as one of the ski-masked men rips it out of his hands. The old lady with the silk scarf turns to run, only to discover that the platform is surrounded. Dozens of figures stand between the stunted trees, watching the commotion from behind goggled eyes.

A woman walks out into the center of the platform. She's not dressed like the others—her boots are black, and she wears a beret instead of a ski mask.

"I want everyone to stand still," she commands, "with your hands up."

The conductor emerges from the little office. "What

is this? What's going on?"

"Which one spotted you?" the woman asks one of the ski-masked men.

He points a gloved finger . . .

At you.

Your heart leaps into your mouth.

"You guys aren't supposed to be using this station anymore," the conductor says. "The train company owns it now."

The woman in the beret ignores him. She walks over to you and holds your gaze with her dark eyes.

"Who did you call?" she asks.

If you tell her you haven't called anyone, go to page 111.

If you bluff, claiming to have called the police, go to page 112.

"I'll catch up with you," you tell Pigeon. She gives you a strange look.

"I'm just going to check something out," you say. Before she has a chance to object, you run across the platform and jump down into the snow, headed for the spot where you last saw the ski-masked man.

There's no sign of him now. Just skeletal trees bending in the scathing wind. You look back toward the train platform, wondering if you've made a mistake—

Then you see the footprints.

They come from shoes much bigger than yours, with crosshatched soles for improved grip. Examining the trail, you conclude that the man walked toward the train station for a while, then turned abruptly and went back. Maybe he saw you looking at him.

You follow the footprints into a thicket of trees. As you push the spiky branches aside, stumbling across the frozen ground, you see a chain-link fence topped with loops of razor wire. Behind the fence is a low building painted white. It would be invisible from a distance or from the air.

Something's going on up here. Someone has built some kind of secret base. But who? And why?

You dig out your phone. No reception. You can't call Pigeon or anyone else.

Suddenly the ski-masked man is visible again, walking toward the base. Behind him, part of the chain-link fence is moving. It's an automatic gate, swinging closed.

You duck through the gap just in time. The gate clangs shut, trapping you inside the compound.

The man is trudging toward the building. You're completely exposed. If he turns to look back, he'll see you crouched beside the chain-link fence. So you run after him, the slush leaking into your shoes. The wailing of the wind conceals the sound of your footsteps—hopefully.

Painted on the side of the white building is a blocky logo and the words *DEPARTMENT OF DEFENSE: DO NOT ENTER*. Why wasn't that sign visible from *outside* the razor-wire fence?

The ski-masked man has reached the white building. He punches some digits into a keypad beside a big steel door. The keypad bleeps and the door clanks. The hinges groan as he pulls it open and disappears into the darkness beyond.

The door starts to swing closed.

If you follow him into the building, go to page 119.

If you stay outside and look for a place to hide, go to page 121.

"I haven't made any calls," you say.

The woman stares at you for a long time.

"OK," she says.

She turns around to address the rest of the group. "You're all going to get back on the train," she says. "Do it quickly and quietly, for your own safety."

You wonder if that's a threat.

"This is preposterous!" the conductor yells. "We have every right to—"

The woman moves so she's standing very close to him. You don't see exactly what she does next, but whatever it is, it makes the conductor stop talking. He gulps like a fish, a vein bulging on his forehead.

"Back on the train," she says again. "Quickly and quietly."

This time no one protests. The camouflage men all release their prisoners. Your hair is suddenly free. You turn to look back, but whoever grabbed you has already melted into the shadows of the platform.

You and Pigeon board the train along with all the other passengers. The conductor shuffles morosely into his little compartment. He doesn't shut the door.

Turn to page 117.

02:18

"**I** already called the cops," you say. "They'll be here soon."

"Is that so?" the woman says. She unlocks your phone. By the time you start wondering how she got it out of your pocket without you noticing and how she knew the code, she's already scrolling through your most recent calls.

"Yes," she says. "That's what I thought."

"I deleted the call record," you say. "For security."

"If that were true, you wouldn't be telling me." She signals the guy behind you, who grabs you by the armpits and drags you across the platform toward the train. You struggle, but he's impossibly strong.

"All of you," the woman yells. "Get back on board the train. This is a restricted area."

The ski-masked man throws you through the open door. You crash down onto the stairs inside.

You had hoped that your bluff would encourage the other passengers to stand up to the goons, but they don't. They just amble sheepishly into the train. The conductor enters his compartment, flops down into his chair, and stares gloomily at the controls.

Pigeon takes your hand and helps you to your feet.

"How do they expect to get away with this?" she asks.

You look out the window. The woman is directing two ski-masked men to open and unload an equipment case. Pigeon's right. There's only one way the soldiers can be sure the passengers won't tell anyone what happened.

You slam your hand down on the CLOSE DOORS button just in time. The doors slide shut just as one of the ski-masked men lifts a grenade out of the equipment case and lobs it toward the train. The grenade hits the doors and bounces back onto the platform. The soldiers scatter.

"Head down the mountain!" you shout. But the conductor isn't in his seat anymore. He's emerged to see what the commotion is about.

There's no time to explain what's going on. You run into the conductor's compartment, trying to remember the images from the train company's website. There had been some pictures of the controls. You look for the lever labeled "brakes."

You see it and wrench the lever upward. The wheels unlock with a *clank*. The train starts rolling backward down the mountain.

"What are you doing?" the driver shrieks.

On the platform, the grenade is spilling clouds of green smoke. The soldiers weren't trying to blow up the train––they intended to gas the passengers.

The driver wrestles for control of the brake. You cling desperately to it. If the train stays here, everyone will die.

The woman in the beret hasn't fled like her men. She's taking two more items out of the equipment case: a gas mask, which she pulls over her face, and a massive gun-shaped object.

She aims at the departing train.

"Get down!" you scream.

BZOWR! A bolt of lightning punches through the train. It doesn't break the window or hit anybody, but all the lights in the train go out. The control monitor flickers and dies. The conductor finally manages to grab the brake lever, but when he pulls it, nothing happens.

All the passengers drop to the floor. The woman on the platform fires the electric gun again. *BZOWR!* Another energy beam blasts through the train, setting one of the seats on fire. Everyone is screaming, including you.

But the train is gaining speed. Already the platform on top of the mountain is shrinking into the distance. Soon the woman and her lethal weapon are just specks, shrouded in green smoke.

"I can't stop the train!" the conductor shouts. He pushes a button and yanks a lever. "The system won't reboot!"

Pigeon is right behind you. "What happens when we hit the bottom?" she asks.

"At this speed? I have no idea, but it won't be good!"

You run out of the conductor's compartment. The

floor shudders as the train hurtles faster and faster down Mount Grave.

"Everyone strap yourselves in!" you yell.

As the passengers scramble to their seats, you notice something out the window—a curved mirror bolted to the side of the train, designed to show the tracks behind the train. The train is racing backward down the slope, so this mirror is the only way to see what's up ahead.

You can see a Hummer—an oversized four-wheel drive—chugging up the tracks, a cloud of exhaust pooling behind it.

As you watch, two men leap out of the Hummer. One is a huge man in a suit, the other is an old guy in a golf cap. They scramble away from the car, leaving it idling on the tracks.

There's no way to stop the train. All you can do is jump into your seat next to Pigeon and fasten your seatbelt.

Smash! The train hits the Hummer like a sledge-hammer. You jerk backward in your seat. In the mirror, you can see the Hummer sliding down the rails, stuck to the back of the train.

And you can see what's ahead: the platform at the bottom of the mountain, complete with great big wooden buffers. Those are supposed to stop an out-of-control train; but you doubt the engineers had this particular scenario in mind.

Pigeon has seen it too. "Hold on tight!" she yells.

BOOM!

The impact pushes you down into your seat. The Hummer absorbs a lot of the force—it gets crushed between the train and the buffers like a soda can under a combat boot. The buffers crumple. All the windows of the train car smash. The walls bend in zigzag patterns, like an accordion.

Finally everything stops moving. The echoes of the crash die away. You look around at all the other passengers in stunned silence. Everyone seems to be OK.

"I've been thinking," Pigeon says finally. "How about next time we just go to surf camp?"

00:00

You survived! There are ten other ways to escape the danger— try to find them all!

"**I** don't get it," Pigeon whispers. "How can they expect to get away with this?"

"Seems like a dumb way to keep a secret," you agree. "They must know we'll tell everyone as soon as we get back."

The doors start to slide shut. Through the window you watch as one of the camouflage men approaches the train. Just as the doors are about to close he tosses something through the gap into the train.

It's a small matte-gray canister, spilling clouds of green smoke.

Tear gas!

Someone screams. You and Pigeon scramble out of your seats and down the aisle toward the other end of the train, desperate to outrun the toxic mist. The other passengers around you are doing the same.

But you're suddenly so tired. Your limbs seem to weigh hundreds of pounds. You can barely keep your eyes open.

"Not tear gas," you say, "Sleep gas. Forget . . . gas . . ."

You were going to say more, but now you can't remember what you were talking about. You're not sure who you were running from, or even where you are.

"Pigeon," you hear yourself say, but you're not sure why. Is there a pigeon in the train car?

How did you get here, anyway?

The floor swings up to meet you.

Go to page 1.

You slip into the gloom just before the door clangs shut. As your eyes adjust, you see the ski-masked man walking away up a corridor with smooth concrete walls and fat power cables snaking along the ceiling.

You're inside. But inside what?

"Sedrick!" A woman's voice. "Where have you been?"

You quickly duck out of sight around a corner, heart pounding. Hopefully the woman didn't see you.

"Outside," the ski-masked man says. "A train full of people came up the mountain—I wanted to make sure they weren't here to interfere."

"And were they?"

"No. Just sightseers."

"I hope they didn't sightsee anything they weren't supposed to," the woman says darkly.

"I don't think so. We're good."

Their footsteps are coming closer. If they walk past this side corridor, there's no way they won't see you.

"I thought we arranged for that train to be canceled," the woman is saying.

"Me too. Someone messed up, big time."

You look around. A nearby door is slightly ajar. You could go through, but you might find yourself trapped.

Maybe you should go up the stairs at the end of the corridor instead—but they're made of rickety metal. The man and the woman might hear you.

"Should we postpone the second test?" Sedrick is asking.

"Are you kidding?" the woman says. "The machine is already warming up. Shutting it down now would cost tens of thousands of dollars. Besides, we have to find out right away if it's possible to send the item back. We press on."

If you slip through the door, go to page 124.

If you go up the stairs instead, go to page 125.

The door falls shut before you have time to reconsider. You flatten yourself against the wall and contemplate your next move.

Looking back at the fence, you can't see a way out. The automatic gate seems to be locked now. The razor wire would shred your hands if you tried to climb over, the snow would freeze them off if you tried to tunnel under. Plus there's probably concrete underneath.

But presumably other people will be coming and going. You just need to follow them out—and stay hidden between now and then.

You look back at the door the ski-masked man went through. You can't stay here. If someone comes out, they'll see you—

And then you spot the security camera. Perched above the door like a curious crow, its black lens pointed right at you.

You turn to run—

But it's too late.

An alarm blares through the compound. It sounds like an air-raid siren. You half expect a nuclear weapon to drop out of the sky.

Boots thud in one direction. Dogs bark in another.

You can't see anyone yet, but in seconds you'll be surrounded.

You sprint toward the fence. It'll cut up your fingers, but that might be better than being caught.

As you run, you take off your jacket and bundle it around one of your hands. It's the best you can do.

You're almost at the fence when one of the dogs explodes into view—a Rottweiler, galloping toward you on long legs. Its mouth is crowded with slobbery fangs.

You dive for the fence, but you're too slow. You've barely grabbed the chain-link when the dog bites your pant leg and pulls you back down off the fence.

Hitting the snow knocks the air out of your lungs. The dog pins you down with one massive paw and growls in your ear.

"Sergei! Down."

The dog releases you and, grinning like a puppy, trots over to an approaching soldier. The man is dressed head-to-toe in white camouflage fatigues. Mirrored glasses conceal his eyes.

He scratches the dog behind the ears. "What are you doing here?" he asks you.

"I was on the train," you stammer. "I saw someone walking around near the platform, and I went to get a better look, and then I got trapped inside the fence."

"Uh-huh." He doesn't sound like he believes you.

"Please. I just want to go home."

He helps you to your feet. "And you can," he says. "But not right away."

"What do you mean?"

He leads you over to the white building and presses the numbers on the keypad to unlock the door. "Well," he says, "I don't know how much you've seen."

"Nothing," you say quickly.

He pushes you through the door into a concrete corridor. "So we can't let you go," he says, "until we've finished our activities here. At that point, it won't matter what you saw or didn't see."

"But I didn't see anything!"

He nods understandingly and opens another door. "Through here, please."

In the room beyond there is a mattress and a stainless steel toilet. By the time you realize the soldier has led you into a prison cell, he's already closing the door behind you.

"See you in two years," he says.

"Two *years*?!"

The lock clanks shut.

THE END.

For another try, go back to page 130.

01:41

You dive through the gap and close the door behind you, muffling the two voices. The room is small and circular, with plastic laminated walls. A spiderweb of power cables dangles from the ceiling.

There's no way out. You just closed the only door.

In the center of the room is a raised platform with a single shoe on it. It's old-fashioned but unworn, with thin black laces and crisp, shiny leather sides.

It's such an odd thing to find in this strange round room that you can't help but stare. You pick up the shoe and turn it over, as though something is going to be written on the hard rubber sole. But there's nothing—not even a price sticker.

Something hums above you. Looking up, you see that the power cables are starting to light up at the joins. It's like staring up at a sky full of stars—

Really hot stars. You're suddenly sweating.

Whatever is about to happen, it's bad. Maybe you'd be better off getting caught.

You're about to scream for help when all the stars rush inward and there's a mighty *ZAP*—

Turn to page 127.

You race up the staircase, your feet near the edge of each step so they don't clang too loudly. Sedrick and the woman keep chatting in the corridor behind you. It doesn't sound like they've heard you.

But you're trapped. At the top of the stairs is a wall, featureless except for a small maintenance hatch, bolted closed.

The stairs rattle. Someone is coming up after you.

You crouch down beside the hatch and yank on the bolt. It's not locked. Once it's out of the way, you pull the hatch open and wriggle into the crawl-space behind it.

The tunnel is pitch-black and rubbery, lined with dozens of power cables. There's no room to reach back and close the hatch behind you. All you can do is crawl forward into the darkness and hope whoever is coming up the stairs doesn't see your feet.

"Hey!" Sedrick calls.

You freeze.

"Did you leave the access hatch open?"

"I don't think so," the woman calls back.

Sedrick grunts and slams the door closed. You hear him sliding the bolt into position, sealing you in.

Don't panic, you tell yourself.

Maybe there's a way out at the other end.

You crawl deeper into the tunnel, trying not to sneeze as concrete dust tickles your nostrils. The power cables remind you of eels. And is it your imagination, or are they humming?

It's definitely hot in here. Your collar is sticking to your neck.

More voices, from somewhere below.

"How long until transmission?" someone is saying.

"Six seconds," someone else says. "Five. Four—"

The hum is getting louder now. It's like a beehive just behind your head. Your hair stands on end, charged. Something is burning the back of your neck. You go to brush it away and sparks shower down around you. Whatever they're testing down below, it requires a huge amount of power—and you're stuck in the middle of the circuit!

"Two," the voice says. "One."

BZZZZZT. The whole world vanishes like a TV switching off.

THE END.

For another try, go back to page 130.

52,560,106:55

"Argh!" You cover your face with your arms, but the heat is suddenly gone. So is the humming. You can't hear anything but jingling, like sleigh bells. The air smells different too—a farmy odor. Like horse poop.

"Santa?" you say stupidly.

But when you uncover your face, it's not Santa. It's a man in a brown coat, a cream shirt, and a bowler hat. He's just walked in through a glass door with a wooden frame, nudging the little bells dangling above it. He looks at you as though you're mad.

You're in a shop. You turn around slowly. A shoe shop. Racks and racks of shoes surround you, all leather, even the children's sizes. They range in color from black to brown. The floor is varnished wood. Sawdust fills the cracks.

"Is it your intention to buy that?" a voice says.

You turn around. The shopkeeper—a moustachioed man in a gray apron—is glaring at you.

"Because I don't think it will fit you," he continues.

You look down and realize you're still holding the shoe from the round room. You drop it. It clatters against the floor.

"You'd best be off," the shopkeeper says sternly.

You push past the man in the bowler hat, who still hasn't said a word. The door bells jingle as you pull the door and step out into the open air.

It's not a proper street. There are no streetlights, no telephone poles, and no asphalt—just tightly packed dirt. You watch in amazement as four horses trot past, snuffling and snorting. That explains the smell. Behind them, a driver with a whip is perched atop a stagecoach. Through the coach window you can see a woman in a dress with puffy sleeves, her veil half concealed by an enormous hat.

You're getting dizzy. You sit down on the dirt as the awful truth dawns. You've survived the train, the mountain, and the ski-masked men . . .

. . . but now you're stuck in the past.

THE END.

Go back to page 130 to try again.

You race forward, your blood thick with adrenaline, and throw yourself through the gap . . .
The top half of you makes it.

THE END.

For another try, go back to page 90.

06:13

You can't see much. The valleys far, far below are concealed by a blanket of clouds that look almost solid. It feels like you could jump off a cliff and land safely on the cotton-ball waves.

You dig out your compass. You had heard from someone that the needle would spin around and around because of the altitude, but it doesn't.

Suddenly you realize someone is standing on the mountain. A man dressed entirely in white, from his boots to his ski mask.

Camouflage. It looks like he's staring at you—but you can't be sure, because the train sweeps into the station, cutting off your view.

The train stops so suddenly you jolt forward in your seat.

"I'm going into the station to use the radio," the conductor says. "I'll need everyone to disembark. I recommend taking a look from the observation platform—if the wind picks up and clouds move on, the view will be spectacular."

"If the wind picks up we'll all freeze," Pigeon grumbles. But she obediently shuffles off the train along with everyone else.

The platform is even shabbier than the one at the bottom of the mountain. Scrunched up balls of paper hop along the concrete like tumbleweeds. There's a vending machine with no power, and a map covered in too much graffiti to read.

This is supposed to be the maiden voyage of this train, but the platform looks like it has been here a long time. So who built it, and why?

The conductor gets out of the train and trots over to an unmarked door on the far side of the platform. He unlocks it and disappears inside.

Pigeon is saying something, but you're not listening. You can see the man in the ski mask again, trudging through the snow toward the platform. He's much closer than he was before.

A gust of wind comes up and the man disappears in a cloud of snowflakes and mist.

"Huh?" you say.

"I said, let's go this way," Pigeon says, pointing to the conductor's office. "Out of the wind."

You look back at the slope, but you can't see the man anymore.

If you follow Pigeon into the shelter behind the office, go to page 106.

If you go to investigate the man in the ski mask, go to page 109.

10:01

You try to make your case, but the conductor waves you off.

"That's a decision for me," he says, "not you. Now you kids get back. I wasn't kidding about that fire."

You and Pigeon trudge back over the stones and snow to where the other passengers are huddled like penguins.

"Hey," Pigeon says. "Look."

You follow her gaze to a dark spot in the sky. "Is that a helicopter?"

"It sure sounds like one."

Now that she mentions it, you can hear the swirling blades—a distant *whopping* sound.

You wave your arms above your head. "Hey!" you shout. "Down here!"

If you can get their attention, maybe they'll land. Then you can ask them to fly down the mountain and search for that boy. The one you didn't save.

But to the pilot, you must just look like a pinprick in the snow. The helicopter drones away, out of sight behind the mountain.

Pigeon puts a hand on your shoulder. "It was worth a try," she says.

"Everybody back on board!" the conductor shouts.

The other passengers shuffle toward the train.

Did you try to convince the conductor to go back down the hill?
Turn to page 69.

If you told him to drive to the top instead, go to page 54.

00:43

"**I**'m in," you say.

The woman laughs. "Can you believe this kid?"

"You know I only pick the best," the man says as he clambers into the helicopter. He ruffles your hair like an affectionate uncle. "Welcome to the team."

The woman thumps on the wall to alert the pilot. "Good to go!" she shouts. "Back to base."

The helicopter wheels around and carries you away to your new life as a bandit.

THE END.

Go back to page 81 to try again.

"No way," you say.

The man laughs as he hauls himself into the helicopter. "She's just kidding. You don't get a choice—you're one of us now." He thumps on the wall to alert the pilot. "We're all on board! Time to refuel."

The helicopter sweeps around, taking you away to start your new life as a bandit.

THE END.

Go back to page 81 to try again.

09:21

You don't like the way those bushes are rustling outside the entrance. You step away cautiously, deeper into the mine.

"Where are you going?" Taylor hisses.

You shush him. You keep one hand on the wall as you fumble through the blackness of the shaft—

And then suddenly the ground disappears from beneath your shoes. You've walked into a hidden pit.

You barely have time to scream before you tumble forward, arms windmilling, feet kicking helplessly.

You fall farther and farther, faster and faster, your panicked breaths echoing around the tunnel, just long enough to realize that there's no way you can possibly survive the impact—

Wham!

THE END.

For another try, go back to page 52.

You turn back toward the entrance. It's definitely time to get out of here—

And suddenly you see it.

A shape, emerging from the shadows in the tunnel. It's bigger than a dog. A wolf, maybe, with thick shaggy legs and sharp fangs shining in the dark.

Then it stands up on its hind legs, impossibly huge, and you finally realize what you glimpsed out the window of the train—

A bear!

The bear roars, spit flying from between its jagged jaws. It must be ten feet tall and at least six hundred pounds. There's no way to fight it.

"Run!" you shout, and dive for the entrance.

But Taylor is too slow. The beast snags his leg with a fearsome claw. Taylor screams as the bear drags him back into the darkness. His fingernails leave trails in the dirt.

If you try to help him, go to page 57.
If you save yourself, go to page 58.

Y ou tear the zipper down. It gets stuck about halfway, but that still leaves you with enough room to get your head through. You fall out of the coat and plummet toward the ground, stomach churning, the freezing wind scraping at your skin.

The ice rushes up to meet you. You brace yourself.

Crash!

You smash *straight through* the sheet of ice and find yourself underwater! That explains why the ground was so flat—in summer, this must be a pond. The cold fluid soaks straight through your clothes, stinging your skin all over.

You scream. Bubbles of precious air explode out of your mouth and dance away toward the surface. You try to swim upward, but your limbs are already frozen. They won't obey your commands.

The hole in the ice above you gets farther and farther away, and soon there's nothing but cold blackness.

THE END.

To try again, go back to page 81.

You stretch out your hands, grabbing for the trees as they rush toward you. The pointed branches get closer and closer, ready to scratch out your eyes—

Success! You grab a sturdy branch and hang on tight.

The helicopter thunders past overhead. The rope gets tighter and tighter, choking you, and then—

Rip! The hood tears off your coat. The grappling hook drifts away, a scrap of fabric dangling from it.

Breathing heavily, you clamber down the tree and drop to the ground. You made it! You didn't get crushed under a train, impaled in a tree, or murdered by bandits.

Now it's time to go home. You start walking down the hill, savoring the fresh air in your lungs.

00:00

You survived! There are ten other ways to escape the danger— try to find them all!